T0160706

Philosophie Thinly Clothed

Philosophie Thinly Clothed

and other stories

Heather Folsom

Cadmus Editions
San Francisco

Philosophie Thinly Clothed and other stories copyright © 2002 by Heather Jean Folsom

Printed in the United States of America
Distributed by Publishers Group West
This book is printed on acid-free paper

Cover illustration: adapted from Philosophie am Himmel by A. Shapiro, with permission

First Edition / 2003

Cadmus Editions
Belvedere-Tiburon
California
www.cadmus-editions.com
e-mail: cebiz@cadmus-editions

Folsom, Heather Jean
Library of Congress 2002104985
ISBN 0-932274-60-9

10   9   8   7   6   5   4   3   2

Contents

Philosophie Thinly Clothed

The House of Inspection

LONG AGO A PRISON WAS DESIGNED, the Panopticon. Prisoners would be isolated in separate cells that were organized like a stack of rings around a central tower. By special devices the inspector in the tower would be able to see each prisoner but the prisoners would not be able to see the inspector. The prisoners could never be certain whether they were being watched or not. This combination of isolation and the sense of being observed was to lead to moral reflection and rehabilitation. Versions of the Panopticon have been constructed from time to time; the latest and most uncompromising was the experimental women's prison at A——.

I awoke in despair. Outside the window that was the transparent inner wall of my cell, the obsidian black of the Tower greeted me with its impenetrable gaze. Another aimless day began.

I was used to austerity. A spy, I had thrived on it, alone and patient. In those days I had been the hidden one; concealment was my pleasure and my power. Now I was the one who was spied upon, by unseen guards within the Tower. Microphones detected every sound. It was unbearable. My only wish was for suicide, which, of course, was denied me. I could not force myself to get up. I closed my eyes again.

At that moment I heard something new: a faint rasping coming from somewhere in the wall beside my bed. I have perfected the art of impassivity; I gave nothing away, though my thoughts and pulse were racing. Had privation driven my senses over the edge into hallucination? Was this some experiment emanating from the Tower? Or could it possibly be something outside its implacable order? After awhile the rasping stopped. Whatever its cause, the novelty gave me the strength to get up.

I forced myself to stay away from the wall and go through my daily routine. Eventually night came; the light in my cell remained on, as always. Lying down I heard the sound again. It now seemed more like scratching or scraping which stopped and started from time to time.

The next day was altogether different. There was no scratching to greet me when I awakened, but I felt hungry, thirsty, exquisitely impatient. I made every effort to appear unchanged, to mask my feelings of anxiety and excitement. At last it was time to lie down again. The blessed, mysterious noise had returned.

The episodes of scratching continued for several days. One night there was a momentary change in pitch: it went up, then there was silence. I rolled over next to the wall as if turning in sleep. An almost imperceptible hole had appeared. I watched it through half-lidded eyes.

A few nights later something tiny and spherical emerged from the hole, rolled a little distance, and came to rest on the floor. Was it possible the prisoner in the cell next to mine had succeeded in a gamble of contact? Could the object be dangerous? My only fear was that it would be taken away.

I let a couple of days go by. Then, dropping a piece of bread on the sphere, I was able to unobtrusively pick it up. I looked at it on my tray. Not knowing what to do, I put it in my mouth. When it came in contact with a tooth, there was a vibration. I pushed on it more firmly.

I felt a pattern of long and short pulses, a simple code I had learned in childhood. But the message now was like nothing I had heard before.

It was a barrage of rantings of every description, delivered at a tremendous pitch of intensity. There were outpourings of prejudice and hatred, fantasies of violence accompanied by curses and epithets, psychotic rhapsodies, monologues of suicide and self-mutilation. Every possible perverse act was described. I stayed awake at night and spent my days bathed in the stream of words. What was the source of this mayhem? Could it be my jailers? It seemed impossible, such an intense pressure of expression from the faceless desolation of the Tower. If this were some new form of mind control, I chose to submit.

Eventually I tapped my tongue against the sphere. The current of language flowed on, ignoring me. I attempted to interject myself several times. At last I succeeded in getting out a complete phrase.

Suddenly there was a response, a curse at my stupidity, but nonetheless, a reaction from some unseen soul. My gratitude surprised and frightened me. I retreated into listening.

I began to recognize others: some by their characteristic turns of phrase; some by their familiar rhythms and hesitations; and some, of course, by their signature preoccupations. A few gave their names, most went by pseudonyms.

There was no limit to the violence of the ravings. It seemed to fill a desperate need, beyond reaction to the misery of imprisonment, to something deeper: a demand for complete exposure and understanding. What would have happened if the speakers had been able to confront each other in person? Fights to the death, I supposed. The exchanges replaced something essential that had been utterly exhausted during months and years of isolation. The dark—even detestable—passions of others were better than the vacuum of one's own depleted imagination. Newcomers were easy to recognize, as hesitancy and restraint gave way to fluency and freedom beyond reckoning.

We were all sentenced to life without parole, a fact that haunted every waking moment. The arrogant Tower believed it knew its captives, and in knowing us, controlled us. But the hidden world of words was our truer life, which the Tower, for all its vigilance, never suspected. This world was our deliverance.

Over time the colloquy changed. Crimes were confessed, tales told. A few of us were more reticent; I seemed to be the most reserved of all. Once in awhile I would make a comment. Occasionally I even revealed a story from my past.

Gradually, almost imperceptibly, something happened to me: for the first time I began to feel that I was part of something. I was repelled and drawn closer at the same time. I followed with interest the lives of each prisoner. I awakened each morning in the river of narrative; I fell asleep in it at night.

So much was shared, and so continuously, it came to feel like the sharing of thought itself, unalloyed by inhibition or even by language. All this at A——, the most unlikely place on earth, and therefore the most necessary.

The tenor of our reflections continued to change. Now there were occasions of agreement: the yearning for freedom, the dread of death, the haunting of regret. At times a melancholic mood, bordering on despair, descended on us. There were even periods of silence—not because we were absent but because we had no words for our grief. We were profound, foolish, brilliant, wrong, vulnerable, our greatest and worst selves. There was time for everything. Ultimately, there was an expectation of everything.

Breakout was a topic that was discussed in a variety of ways, most commonly as a joke, an impossible hope. Suddenly we became electrified with the idea, unified and passionate. A tremendous craving burst forth, to see beyond the Tower to a city, a stretch of desert, a mountain. The talk was of nothing else: what was missed, what was dreamed of, and finally, how it would be done. The risk was great. We faced the loss of our salvation, communication itself. But such was our longing, we agreed to go forward.

We embarked on a program of distractions, taking turns enacting crises that required attention from the Tower. At a designated time, a few prisoners would stage attempted suicides, heart attacks, psychotic episodes. Simultaneously, other prisoners would work on weakening the walls between the cells and on the more difficult walls that bordered the outer corridors. We drilled and scraped with the most primitive of tools. We constantly commented on our progress, shared frustrations and warnings, offered advice.

When it was my turn to create a distraction, an attack upon the hated inner wall which was to end with injuring my leg, I threw myself into the task without reservation. Others cheered me on. I signaled for them to stop, fearing my performance might be compromised. Everyone became silent. The profundity of that silence, the camaraderie and presence of it, stopped my breath.

The time for breakout was near. We had a rapid count-off system for checking in. We had backup plans: anyone could ask for help; if someone missed three check-ins in a row, a rescue group would be sent to that location. We practiced and drilled until everything was automatic.

The night before the breakout we feigned sleep but held a giant party. We became sentimental, silly, told jokes and stories. We knew we should rest but we were too excited. There was apprehension: what if it were all a hoax? What if we failed?

Though I was nervous and tired the next morning, I forced myself to eat breakfast as usual. It suddenly occurred to me that I would soon be viewing the others whose disembodied minds I now knew as well as my own. I worried that we might appear different to the eyes in the Tower. I lounged, tried to look re-laxed, felt particularly exposed. We were subdued, mostly silent. From time to time someone blurted out an anxious thought.

We were well into the final check-in round, ready for our roles in the breakout. The moment came. We attacked the walls between the cells, vulnerable from months of surreptitious drilling. The walls crumbled. Groups formed in designated cells and hurled them-selves against the weakened outer walls; they gave way in jagged sections. Still communicating only by the spheres, we awaited the arrival of the guards.

As we had expected, not enough guards were sent.

It had seemed unlikely that the Tower would be prepared for a complete uprising. After all, the principle
of the prison was isolation. Not even the all-seeing
Tower could have guessed the unanimity of our effort. We heard shouts of surprise and disbelief.

Another contingent of guards arrived but it was too
late and there were still too few of them. We heard
their exclamations but we did not speak. This seemed
to further unhinge them. We bound and left them—
without a word.

Upon reaching the ground level, the unexpected
happened: in one body we turned, not outside to
freedom, but inside. We were impelled toward the
Tower, to enter the structure that had oppressed us
for so long.

We surged into a vast cylinder of a room. From
the inside its curved wall was transparent. A ramp
spiraled upward, dotted every ten yards or so with
an observation guard-post. At the posts, overturned
chairs gave evidence of the haste with which the guards
had fled. In the center of the room the empty superintendent's chair slowly rotated. We rushed up to the
posts, each of us driven to find our cell.

I found mine. There were the holes in my walls
made only moments before. There were the guards,

still bound. They were writhing in confusion in the empty, ravaged cells.

We too were confused. At the culmination of our attack, standing at the observation posts and looking back at our cells, a strange quietude gripped us. Astonishingly, it seemed to be regret at our incipient parting.

A moment later a sense of urgency coursed through us. We ran to the underground garage and climbed into transport vans and staff cars, snatching available clothing as we went. I managed to grab a civilian jacket. We started the engines, opened the doors, and headed out.

In the nearest city I jumped down from the van and signaled my good-byes. The van went on. I removed the sphere from my mouth and put it in my pocket. The change was as shocking as a fall into icy water. I was alone.

Familiar patterns of survival returned. I got money and checked into a hotel. Then, just when I expected to be most active and purposeful, I lost all energy. I stayed in the hotel room, ordering from room service, sleeping, reading newspapers, and watching TV for news of the breakout. Nothing. There were sounds all around me, yet the world seemed unnaturally silent. I started talking angrily to myself, "Have you turned into one of those prisoners who can't make it on the outside?" But I could not overcome my inertia, nor could I stop wondering why there was no mention of the breakout.

Cursing myself for my foolishness, I went back toward A——. I stayed across the valley and watched the prison through binoculars. For several days no one went in or out. Unable to contain my curiosity any longer, I made my way to the prison.

The gates to the garage were unlocked. A few vehicles were inside but there was no sign of activity. My new gun drawn, I advanced into the garage and took a staircase up to the Tower.

At first the huge cylinder seemed unchanged. The chairs were still overturned at the observation posts; the room appeared empty.

I heard a voice. Someone in a guard uniform was rotating in the superintendent's chair and talking on the telephone. She hadn't noticed me. She seemed to be indicating that everything was functioning normally. She hung up.

I crept behind her and placed my gun against her head. She seemed, inexplicably, bored. She waved a hand toward the ramp.

To keep my gun in place, I had to circle alongside

the chair. Was some trap being set? Did the Tower still hold some covert power?

The phone rang and the guard answered. Again she was reporting that all was as usual. When she hung up, I jerked the gun sharply against her head and asked for an explanation. Instead of answering, she sighed, got up, and started to walk over to the ramp. Momentarily, I flicked my eyes away from her and out toward the cells. I could hardly believe what I saw.

The walls were still in shambles but the scene was transformed. Many cells were jammed with furniture. Some cells contained two, even three, occupants.

The guard continued toward the ramp; I was right behind her. She started to raise her hand. I grabbed it and pinned it behind her back. She cursed and told me she was trying to point to her mouth.

Of course.

I put my hand in my pocket, found the sphere, and positioned it in place. In that instant of relief, I knew: the river of rhythms, the connection of mind and word, had become a necessity to me. I was shocked at the intensity of my reaction. I started trembling.

But something discordant was present, a cacophony of novices and strangers. It was the babble of early days: hatreds, misunderstandings, depravities.

I broke in and demanded to know what was going on. Greetings swarmed back at me.

I was further undone, almost weeping. Someone I knew explained that nearly everyone had returned and taken up residence in their old cells. The newcomers were guards and prison personnel, even the superintendent.

I ran up the ramp and looked out to my cell. Two interlopers had made it their home. I announced that I was returning. Some activity began in the cell but it wasn't fast enough to suit me. I added, more forcefully, they had five minutes to clear out. I reminded everyone that I was a loner.

In response the sphere pulsed wildly, its version of hoots of laughter.

Above the Gorge

THE TWO MOUNTAINS WERE SO NARROW and close together, they were referred to by the space between them, the gorge. They were beautiful spikes with cypress trees clinging to their tops and steep sides.

The great poet of the age, Li Dian, saw the spiky mountains in a painting. She came to the gorge and saw them in reality. They took her breath away. She desired to live in the peaks that dressed and undressed in the clouds.

She chose one of the mountaintops and built a series of wooden ladders, stairs, and toeholds to reach it. Then she built a hut at the summit among the cypress trees.

One day Li Dian was sitting at her table, brush in hand, working on a poem. She was vaguely distracted by unusual sounds that seemed to be echoing their way up from below. It was cloudy outside; all she could see was whiteness.

For several days the clouds remained while the sounds grew louder. They seemed to be coming nearer. "What is it?" she wondered.

Li Dian looked out her window one morning and the

clouds were gone. There was a hut on the other peak!

This is what had happened. The other great poet of the age, Pan Qingzao, heard what Li Dian had done and came to see the gorge for herself. When she saw the mountains she was filled with a desire to live on the uninhabited peak. She constructed ladders, stairs, and toeholds, and built a hut of her own.

That first morning Li Dian looked across to the other peak several times. She saw, through the window of the opposite hut, a woman seated at a table, holding brush and paper.

Li Dian had wanted solitude but she felt pleased to have a quiet neighbor nearby. Time passed for the poets in the sky, alone and yet near each other.

One evening Li Dian stood and began shouting a poem to her neighbor. Pan Qingzao looked up in surprise. But after so many days in silence, the sound of a voice was welcome. And this was not just any voice, it was the great Li Dian, reciting a new poem.

When the poet finished, Pan Qingzao responded by calling out a new poem of her own. Li Dian was amazed. For the first time she recognized who was living beside her.

From that day on, the poets would yell their poetry across the gorge. Sometimes there was nothing for them to see but the white world of clouds; sometimes the clouds would part and they would glimpse each other; sometimes, oil lamps in hand, they shouted toward a tiny light in the darkness.

Poetry rained down on the farmers in the gorge. On overcast days the words seemed to fall from the shrouded sky itself.

Wu Yang, the brilliant language scholar at the University, learned of all this. A question formed in her mind: how did listening to the great poets affect the farmers who lived at the base of the mountains? Her theory was that the farmers were irritated by the noise and felt resentful and inferior as a result of being subjected to things beyond their understanding. She came to the gorge, built a small hut, and began her research.

"What is it like for you, having to listen to the poets all the time?" Wu Yang was asking a farmer.

"Poetry is part of our lives. I have learned several of the poems, which I often say out loud as I plow behind my ox."

"Does it bother you, having to listen whenever the poets decide to shout?"

"Not at all. I feel blessed."

"Do the others in the gorge feel this way?"

"Oh, yes."

Wu Yang interviewed everyone. Then she went to the fields and listened to the farmers working alone and together. She overheard them quoting entire poems. She observed that the farmers used phrases from the poems in their everyday speech. Sometimes the original meaning of a phrase would be preserved; sometimes the meaning would be changed to refer to a farming task. She found no instances of irritation, resentment, or inferiority.

Wu Yang completed her research and started to pack up her belongings; it was time to return to the University. She intended to write a paper on what she had learned. But she felt odd and heavy; she could barely move. "What is wrong with me?" she wondered.

She rested a few days. Then she thought, "I might as well write the paper while I am here regaining my strength." She felt better immediately. But when her paper was finished and she was again packing to go, the strange malady returned.

Days passed and the illness lingered on. She lay in her hut, listening to the sounds outside. Finally she understood: she did not want to leave. She had grown to love the gorge, the language of the farmers, and the blessings of the poetry.

She stayed on.

After many years Li Dian died. The farmers held a funeral for her and recited her poems. Pan Qingzao died soon after. It was thought she died of a broken heart, missing her friend in the clouds. The farmers held a funeral and recited Pan Qingzao's poetry, too.

Wu Yang recorded these events. Even after the poets were gone she remained in the gorge. Though poetry descended no more, the farmers continued to repeat what they had learned and to use phrases from the poems. It was a comfort and a pleasure.

To this day, remnants of the old ladders, stairs, and toeholds can be found above the gorge. In later paintings of the two mountains, the huts can sometimes be discerned.

The Jeweler

JAE WISHED TO BECOME A JEWELER. Her desire never wavered and only grew with time. To this purpose she dedicated herself, rather like someone who takes religious orders. She eschewed friendship and the whirl of fashion and society. Instead, she studied jewelry-making and worked and saved money toward her goal.

She obtained a studio in the artisan district of the city and the finest tools, metals, and precious stones. She had notebooks full of the designs she had been imagining all her life.

In her studio she would lie in bed with a notebook and sketch the new designs that never ceased to occur to her. Meanwhile, at her worktable her tools and materials sat untouched.

She began to worry about her lack of progress so she started forcing herself to get up and go over to her table. But in that walk of a few steps she would become weak and exhausted. She would sit down and make herself pick up the gold or silver, the rubies, emeralds, or other gems that lay before her. They felt so heavy she could barely lift them. After a few minutes their weight was intolerable. She would put them down and go back to bed and her notebooks.

There were times she felt an impulse to start making jewelry. But instead of letting herself be propelled by the impulse, she would do the opposite: she would see if she could resist. In her mind, only when the compulsion to work became unbearably strong would it be time to begin. Lesser urges were of no merit.

Her strength in resisting, her mastery of it, grew and grew. She could be almost consumed with her desire to make jewelry, yet still not do so. She became a genius of resistance.

No one has heard from her for a long time. Perhaps the impulse to work finally overcame her genius. Perhaps her genius won out.

The Wonderful Cart

OUR TOWN IS ALL ON ONE SIDE of a steep little mountain that rises sharply from a broad plain. We are used to looking downward—or sometimes up above—in order to see what is to come, or what has gone before.

One day we saw below us something strange and frail-looking. It was swaying from side to side in an ungainly arc, slowly climbing into the town. When it was closer we could see it was a most unusual cart. There were poles sticking out of it in all directions, with various wires running between the poles and small banners holding onto the wires.

It is our custom to stand still when something is unfamiliar and wait for it to draw near and explain itself. We did so. After awhile a new aspect of the contraption made itself known: tinkling music was issuing forth. But the pitches were off, the rhythms were bewildering, and the sounds were not made by any instrument we knew.

As the cart came closer and the music grew louder, another emanation enveloped us: strong scents of fresh yeast and baking. Our mouths began to water. If anything could have uprooted us, it would have been this

21

last beguilement of our senses. Even so, we stood firm. The cart reeled its way to a place in front of us and stopped, though it continued to pitch and shudder and the music continued to play.

A little door opened and a woman climbed out. She was perfectly in keeping with the rest of the enterprise. There was no denying that she was bewitching, but a number of things about her were so bizarre, the effect was more disturbing than pleasing: she wore many layers of skirts and scarves; her demeanor was an odd blend of subservience and authority; and, most disconcerting of all, she had a peculiar wide smile and glittering eyes, unfathomable and vaguely threatening.

Perhaps we should have run away right then. What stopped us was not politeness; we were held fast in uneasy fascination. The woman said nothing, but gave a nod and went back into the cart.

She reappeared holding a tray heaped with pastries. They were like none we had ever seen: huge, glistening, sending up a gauzy plume of steam. With sprightly steps she handed them round. A thought occurred— that we might be poisoned or somehow changed forever. Still, an instant later we were biting fiercely into the wondrous treats.

It was the most delicious moment of our lives. The

temperatures were perfect: piping hot pastry with cool beaten cream in the center; each melting on the tongue in a caress of sweetness. The only possible response was to thrust in our teeth again. But between that first and second bite, something occurred, disregarded yet momentous: a capitulation, even a complicity, from which there was no turning back.

As we ate we studied the face of the cream puff woman. Her smile widened until it was almost grotesque. She stood with the tray poised in her hands. It was certainly not due to hunger, but we devoured another round. Then we really did feel sated. The woman nodded gaily, disappeared into the cart, and headed down away from us.

The next day we jigged with impatience as we watched for the cart. When it burst into view we ran toward it. We clamored shamelessly for the woman to come out and give us more pastries. She obliged, silent and grinning broadly.

So it went for several days. She asked nothing of us in return. Our joy was almost perfect—marred, if at all, by incomprehension, a vague sense of something amiss, which was pushed aside in the excitement aroused by this boon in our lives.

Then one day she did not appear. We ran to and

fro, we called out, but there was no cream puff woman. We were desolate. We knew that nothing would ever equal the miraculous cart and its magical offerings. We went to a lookout and waited, squinting in vain down through the town.

The next day, heavy with dread, we returned to the lookout. We spied the cart, undulating near the base of the town. We ran as fast as we could, then pounded on its little door.

The woman stepped out, her smile unchanged. But we were not the same. With tears running down our cheeks, we reproached her. Where had she been? How could she disappear like that? What must we do to make sure such a thing could not happen again? She went back inside. The music stopped, the cart ceased its movements. She reemerged and in the sudden quiet, she spoke.

Her voice was lilting and musical but her words were oddly formal, as if a strained translation from some unknown tongue. She said she was in need of funds and entreated us to bring her whatever we could find. Furthermore, she needed one of us to go into the cart with her, one of us each day.

Someone preceded her through the curious door. It closed, the music started up, the cart began its writhing. The rest of us raced off in all directions. As we ran, it occurred to us that we would do anything she asked of us.

When we returned, she and our companion were just emerging. Our friend looked rather pale. She took our tribute with the same expression that had greeted our tears. Then, at last, there was the handing round of the cream puffs.

It was difficult to find money for her every day but we did the best we could. We sold our most valued possessions, committed little acts of theft, and pleaded for gifts and loans.

Inside the cart it was very cramped. The smell of baking was overpoweringly strong, the music was deafening, the lurching was dizzying.

What happened is what you are imagining. After all, we loved the cream puff woman. There was nothing we would not do for her. It was merely unnerving that she always smiled. If it hadn't been for the pastries, we could not have believed she loved us in return.

When we had brought her everything we could, when each of us had gone into the cart a time or two, she disappeared. We were shocked and miserable. How could she leave us? We never *never* would have left her. We ran to the very top of the mountain and strained our eyes in search of her.

There on the road across the plain was the cart, tinier than a flea circus cart, moving away. We saw it stop and little specks were gathering around it already.

And what became of us? We remembered the taste of the cream puffs and were filled with a terrible feeling, like an illness: a mixture of rage, revulsion, heartbreak, confusion. How preposterous the cart was. How jarring the music. And the pastries—they were too large, too fantastic. It was all a horrible mistake. We had not known, yet we should have known. Why hadn't we run away?

Now we avoid sweet things and music. Something in us is broken. If it mends at all, it will not be for a long time.

The White Tortoise

JUANA STOOD BY THE PIER, A YOUNG GIRL watching the boats come in to unload the catch: fish, lobster, crab, shrimp. The old grandmother came by in her heavy black skirt and greeted her. The girl slowly turned her head toward the old woman, then turned back to the boats without speaking. The seafood merchant looked at *la abuela,* shrugged her shoulders, and jerked her head back and forth, a slight motion, very rapid. The old woman sighed; her skirt swept from side to side down the lane between the merchants. Juana had the familiar feeling of anticipation.

Her cousin ran up to her house and asked her to join the group of girls. They were old enough now: they were going to walk the promenade. Juana shook her head. She was expecting something.

She knew patience, that tightening of muscle when impulse comes, turning into a wash of heat across the body. If you do not move, it passes. No one can see the strength this stillness takes.

Years passed. The certainty that magic was on its way—flagged but did not disappear. She had no lover, no children, no friends, no activity save waiting:

walking along the beach staring out to the horizon. White Tortoise, *tortuga blanca,* they called her.

She swam every day. She was old and death was near. She wondered, "Is the magic never coming, after all?"

The sky is cloudless, the sun beats down. The waves swell in their strong lunar pull.

At last she sees the tortoise, cresting on a wave. She swims out toward it. She climbs onto its back and wraps her arms and legs around the huge white shell. Down into the blue water they plunge, into muted light. Schools of incandescent fish glide alongside them. Then woman and tortoise rise up; they rise higher, inside a great wave. They break through the surface in a fountain of water drops, sparkling in the sunlight. Her long hair is streaming behind her and she is laughing for joy.

The Rat Suit

THERE WERE ONLY TWO TREES but so tall they were, so entwined and bewildering were their branches, she had never seen the forest. Similarly, so dense and over-powering was the forest, she had never been able to discern the trees.

Long ago, two dreams: one sleeping, one waking. In the sleeping dream the girl's pale wrist was bound and the strong rope was tied around the first tree. The rope that held the other wrist was secured around the second tree. The two trees swayed so violently in a high wind, they exerted a terrible pull on each arm. The third force came from the legs, thrashing franti-cally in an effort to escape, with such energy that the body was horizontal, the legs running away in mid-air, increasing the pain.

The daydream was of looking down at her body and seeing the contours and coarse hair of a rat. It was rather horrifying, for she was terrified of rats, especially large ones.

She had never thought to mention either dream, which had disappeared with childhood. If partially remembered, a vague sense of shame attended.

The woman achieved various successes in the world's eyes, and in her own eyes, too. Then, after such a long time, the daydream of the rat body returned. She might be at work or talking to a friend when, without warning, the specter would float in front of her eyes. If she were with others, a self-deprecating smile would momentarily grip her face. If she were alone, she would admonish herself, aloud, to stop. The illusion would recede, only to visit again.

We are all aware of the two theories of human destiny: the first, that we are in control of our thoughts and actions; the second, that these things are dictated by forces unseen, ungovernable. The woman believed in the first theory. Its proof was her life of public and private success. She had searched diligently in order to discover what was considered worthwhile, and subsequently crafted for herself a life of admirable pursuits.

What, then, was the meaning of the rat vision? Perhaps a small trespass of the second theory, an oversight, revealing a lack of vigilance. The distress she felt when the phantom intruded was evidence of her expectations: after all, she ought to have the strength to create herself completely—to embody the sensible, the healthy, the desirable.

She was tireless in her efforts to banish the rat image. Her first strategy was to intensify self-reproach. But the more she berated herself, the more the specter haunted her. Then she experimented with exorcisms: solemn oaths, clapping of hands, slamming of doors. To no avail. Finally, in desperation, she tried welcoming the hallucination whenever it appeared. Not surprisingly, this also failed. Now the fantasy was with her most of every day.

She had friends with whom she exchanged the intimate details of life. Yet despite the domination of her days by the vision, she made no reference to it. She was ashamed to allude to it when it floated into the middle of a conversation. On the rare occasions when it was not present, the problem seemed too bizarre, remote, even trivial, to confide.

She hurled herself into her work, social engagements, cleaning and ordering. Occasionally she would drift into a trance-like state. These episodes were mysterious to her: sometimes the rat image was present, sometimes not. Afterwards there was a feeling of disorientation, of time passed but unaccounted for.

One day, suddenly, there was a solution, a reconciliation of her competent nature and her chimera. She had the idea of fashioning for herself a rat suit, something she could wear—completely alone, of course—which would transform her phantom into everyday reality.

A surge of happiness and desire accompanied this idea, followed by a host of doubts. How could it be done? For it had to be more than a crude costume, it must be utterly convincing. Then there was the matter of secrecy. Where would she construct it? Where would she keep it? What if she were to die unexpectedly and the suit were found among her effects? Her years of careful self-creation would be undone in an instant. Could she obtain a room somewhere under another name?

She discovered there were any number of places for rent where no questions were asked. She settled on a tiny colorless apartment in a run-down part of the city. Once done, a pang of misgiving assailed her. She told herself she was experimenting; she could back out at any time. But it was undeniable, she felt tremendously excited.

In one day she obtained all the necessary materials for the suit: real rat pelts, silk for lining, cotton batting for padding, thread, needles, and other sundries. It was quite late when she returned to the apartment with her packages. She dumped them on the floor, then reluctantly went out for a late dinner with a friend. She did not trust herself to cancel the engagement with the proper regret.

Leaving only for her job and the most pressing social obligations, she settled into the apartment. Sewing and sewing, padding and sewing, the rat suit took shape. She felt at peace. She told herself she might never actually wear the suit; its construction was a worthy effort in itself, art and science combined. Her contentment consisted of two things: first, in creating the suit, she had no one to answer to. She could take as long as she wished, fashion and refashion it until she was satisfied. Second, she was doing what she most longed to do.

She marveled at the reversal that had taken place: a dream had become real, something held in the hand; while her reasoned life, once so consuming and important, faded more and more into the insignificant, the insubstantial, the dreamlike. Though some part of her was alarmed, she was able to ignore the feeling without much difficulty. How could work or friends or anything else compare to the rat suit?

Occasionally she had to return to her old house. The air inside had grown musty and slightly damp. When she was obliged to receive guests for a dinner party, it amused her that no one noticed any change.

She tried on the lining, even the lining with the padding, but once the fur was added she felt squeamish.

Eventually the rat suit was finished. She laid it out on one of the twin beds in the apartment. Her enthusiasm vanished. The suit was altogether unsatisfying. She had an impulse to abandon it downstairs by the garbage cans and leave the apartment forever. Instead, since it was late, she went to sleep.

When she woke up she understood what was wrong: the fur-covered torso was no longer enough. There were no legs, no claws, no tail, no teeth, no head! A complex set of problems had arisen; she was delighted. She immediately began the research for these new constructions.

The engineering of the rest of the rat suit in all its intricacy took up most of the next year. Once in awhile someone would stop by her house and find her gone. She was amused by the rumor that she had a new lover. When she ran into acquaintances, they would comment on how well she was looking, with conspiratorial, questioning glances. She would shrug her shoulders and smile.

At last the rat suit was complete. Even unanimated it had a frightening appearance, lying on its twin bed.

The proportions were accurate; it was large and heavy-looking. She had bought a bottle of champagne to celebrate the occasion. But after all, she felt quite depressed. She fled from the apartment in a state of confusion bordering on despair and returned to her house. She plunged into her old life: calling neglected friends, cleaning, taking on extra work.

One night on her way home from a dinner party, she went to the apartment instead. The scene inside was frozen like an exhibit in a museum. Here was the chair where she used to sit and work so happily; here was the table where tools and materials had leapt so eagerly into her hands. Now everything stared at her reprovingly. She picked up a pair of cold scissors and set them down again. The beds were on the other side of a partition; she could not bring herself to look behind it. The apartment belonged to the monstrous creation and she was no longer welcome.

After that she merely dropped off the rent money in the manager's office. The whole enterprise was degrading and foolish. How could she have done such a thing as the sordid project upstairs? She was a successful woman: admired, sought after, unencumbered, truly at the pinnacle of everything she prized.

But week by week her accomplished life grew more

unbearable. Something momentous, possibly irrevo-
cable, was afoot. For the first time she felt a kinship
with the figures that slunk by in the shadows. She
found herself in unfamiliar neighborhoods at night,
looking up at illuminated windows. Yellowed shades
obscured the rooms behind. Who was within?—at
work on a private passion or living in its fullness or
scarcely yet admitting what it might be.

Certainty came: that if she must, she would move
beyond the quirk, the foible, the eccentricity, to the
borderland where dwelled the perverted, the insane,
the unredeemable. With this knowledge came self-
loathing and relief.

She went to the apartment, locked the door, stripped
off her clothes, and put on the rat suit. It fit as if it
were her own furred skin. She glanced down. Yes,
even more perfect than in her dream, here was the
coarse-haired abdomen. And not only that: here were
long-fingered claws, a scaly tail. She started to lift her
arm, watching in amazement as the impulse for movement caused the raising of this flawless giant rat leg.
She was horrified and triumphant. She had come to
think of the rat suit as a separate object, inert on its
twin bed. But inhabiting it, giving it life, was over-
whelming. She wished she could look in the mirror

in the tiny bathroom but she could not find the courage.

For the next few hours she prowled around the apartment. Growing more accustomed to her new body, she at last went into the bathroom and looked at herself.

She gasped. The great eyes and ears, the quivering snout, the sharp teeth. Magnificent!

She felt an intense desire to go out into the hallway, to display her perfection, so beautiful and terrifying. But what could anyone possibly understand? Someone might react with amusement. That would be intolerable. The same for curiosity, indifference, sympathy, even admiration. On the other hand, revulsion was also unacceptable. Was there no response that could be borne? Would she be forced to keep her secret forever?

Suddenly she knew what she would do: she would go out into the world; she would face whatever came to pass. It was all beyond her control. She would go in a little while but first she would rest. Getting up onto the bed was too cumbersome; she lay down on the floor. It was quite comfortable. She fell asleep.

This time the rat was bound, not the girl. The wind blew, the rope around each foreleg whined and hawed with the frantic swaying of the trees. The hind legs beat the air in a futile attempt at escape. Then the rat moved its head sideways, extended its neck, and began to gnaw the rope tied around one claw. Snap snap snap, the twining elements of rope gave way between the sharp teeth. The rope moaned and broke with a loud report.

One foreleg was freed but the rat felt a searing pain as its weight fell against the other rope, which tightened around the opposite claw. The head turned, the teeth gnashed, snap snap *snap,* and the rat was free.

The head hit the ground with a thud, the hind legs ceased their flailing. There was pain again, racing through the injured head, throbbing in sharp bursts. The rat lurched up, stumbled, rolled over, and got up again, its chest filling with exhilaration. A bracelet of rope still encircling each claw, the rat headed toward the first tree.

With great energy it began to bite the base of the tree. As soon as the teeth sank into the soft bark, the tree howled with pain and rage. Sap bled from the incision. Fiber by fiber chewed the rat through the trunk. The tree flung itself back and forth in great arcs. There was a splitting sound, louder than the wails, and the tree fell.

Without stopping the rat ran to the second tree and bit down sharply into its bark. This tree trembled more than arced and its protest was higher in pitch. The sap came forth, the rat chewed on. Then, with a shriek, this tree, too, fell.

The wind stopped. Everything was silent. The rat looked at its handiwork, blinked. It gnawed the remains of the ropes from its claws. Then it lumbered off in search of food.

The Heroine

THE HEROINE, CHOSEN FOR LIFE, must embody courage and grandeur of spirit. The position confers wealth and acclaim. She must wear the laurel garland, appear at public fêtes, receive adoration and even worship, and be the subject of songs, poems, and statues.

The Heroine was very old and a successor would soon be needed. There were many who aspired to this honor: some were certain of being favored; some felt worthy but knew bad luck would intervene; some hoped to win but did not feel they deserved it. Much deliberation was given to the matter. Contests were held yet no new Heroine was found.

There was a hermit who lived in a cave in the mountains. She had dealings with only two people: the woman who brought firewood in the fall and the woman who brought tea in the spring.

"Have you heard about the search for a Heroine?" asked the woman who brought the firewood.

"No, but it has nothing to do with me," said the hermit.

Several months later the woman who brought the tea said, "The search is growing desperate."

"It has nothing to do with me," said the hermit.

The woman who brought the firewood returned the next fall. "The old Heroine has died. There is a crisis, for a successor still has not been found."

"It has nothing to do with me."

That night the hermit dreamed she was asked to be the Heroine. She was unhappy and refused the role. She argued with herself, saying, "You are strong enough. You can wear the laurel and not be changed."

When she woke up she knew what she must do: she went down into the city and presented herself to be the Heroine. Not long after, she was chosen.

She was covered in garlands and fêted. People lined the streets for parades in her honor, singing praises for her courage and valor. Statues and poems were begun.

The hermit neither loved her new role nor hated it. It was as if the garlands were for her but not for her, the parades and songs were for her but not for her, the poems and statues were for her but not for her.

She lived a long life as the Heroine of the people. She was not changed.

The Watcher

THE BANK WAS BUILT TO IMPRESS its clientele with a sense of permanence. Its base, from street level to twenty feet up, was masoned in deep green marble, flecked and veined with black and gray.

Halfway along the southern side, the wall is breached by a small structure. This is M's home. Sides and roofs, doors and windows, floors and furnishings continually evolve. Plywood, cardboard, rusted metal, crumbling fiberboard, mattresses and rugs come and go. Her marble back wall, however, imparts a steadfast strength.

I know M as profoundly as it is possible to know another person, better than she could know herself, better, in fact, than I will ever know myself. I fill notebooks with information about her; they go back a long time. I have come to think of myself as her guardian, though she does not know of my existence. I do not meddle. I have observed her so closely and for so long, I am able to know her thoughts. It is my vocation.

I obtained a degree at a women's college and became a schoolteacher. All went well until complaints were lodged that I took too great an interest in my students. This was untrue. I never said a harsh word or did anything improper. If at recess I stood and gazed at the children while other teachers smoked and gossiped, if I sometimes followed students home to see where they lived, what was the harm in that? All my efforts were in order to become a better teacher. Eventually I was hounded into resigning.

I received an unexpected offer: the mother of one of my former pupils would pay me to locate her missing sister. I quickly found her. That was how I began my career as a private investigator. I gained a reputation and my license. I loved stakeouts most of all. I was successful and happy.

Then problems began. When an assignment was completed, I was expected to move on. However, I continued to observe and collect information on former cases. I was warned, reprimanded, placed on probation, and finally required to surrender my license. For awhile I was sent some under-the-table business. Then even that declined, until I no longer had enough money for rent and was forced to live on the street. I expected it would be temporary but I discovered it suited me well. I have no interest in wine cellars, gardens, or the thousand other distractions that consume most people's lives. Even when I had a home, I wanted to be out viewing others.

One afternoon I was walking through the financial district when I came upon the diminutive structure abutting the bank. I was gripped by the sensations of intense curiosity and determination that have guided so many of my actions. I crossed to the other side of the street and waited.

It was growing dark when a woman dressed in a tumbling assortment of clothes went into the little dwelling. Moments later, candlelight flickered inside. I approached, pleased by the many gaps in the walls through which I might observe.

That evening our contract was made: she, unknowingly, to provide a purpose for my life; I, to faithfully watch and chronicle hers.

Early the next morning I constructed my own small residence nearby. Then I was back at work. The woman was on the wide steps of the bank, patiently begging, by ten o'clock. I searched her home while she was out. I found some tattered photographs and a social security card.

I was able to trace her entire life from these objects. I know her history in great detail but I shall be brief. M was from a poor rural family. She excelled in school. She was about to enter college on a scholarship when family illness required her to remain at home. She worked at various jobs and later became a private tutor. At this she was highly successful, becoming indispensable to a series of wealthy families. Then, while still a young woman, she suffered a stroke. Afterwards she remained impaired. She had a few jobs as a maid but even those she could not perform adequately, due to her problems with comprehension. A former employer placed her in an expensive nursing home. She hated it and ran away. She wound up in the city, where she found the bank, built her house, and began her new life.

One cold morning several months ago I was at my post. On her way to the bank steps, M came upon a large object lying darkly on the sidewalk. She understood this to be an omen and went to considerable trouble to move it into her home. At first she used it as a table. Later it occurred to her that it was a television and she might be able to watch it.

She went looking for inspiration. She encountered a street gang. Loud music was coming from a machine of some kind. She saw wires coming from the machine and going into a phone booth. One of the gang members saw M go into the booth. When she understood what M wanted, she tried to show her how the wires were attached to the front of the payphone.

M could not follow what she was saying. The gang walked over to M's home and hooked up her TV.

M watched television only at night when the street was empty. She looked forward to it all day. An inner emptiness, of which she had not been aware, was replaced with a new world of flickering images. A wonderful strangeness filled her thoughts: pyramids, monkeys, the Taj Mahal, beer cans. She saw earrings, teeth, dinosaurs, chairs, soap, insects. She began to comprehend some of the events that were being shown: these women were going away on a huge boat; this horse could run very fast.

Her understanding deepened. Then her companion began to turn on her. She had assumed that people who lived in big houses felt trapped and were not happy, like those she had left behind in the nursing home. But on TV many of the people in big houses were laughing and smiling. When she saw people like herself, who lived in small houses on the street, they were the ones who were not happy. Every night brought fresh pain: this woman lived in a huge mansion and laughed all the time; this one had everything she could want—dazzling clothes of every color, many televisions. The only thing M had to be proud of was her marble wall, but it was no longer enough.

Perhaps it did not even belong to her. Everything in her life seemed hopelessly shabby. Her days filled with anguished longings.

Television revealed that others had these longings, too. TV began to teach her how to obtain the things she now desired. You could get things, not by politely waiting for them to be given to you or by looking through garbage cans, but by methods she had never considered: saying you were a church and should be sent money, but M could not speak so well; selling a lotion for the hair or the skin, but M had nothing to sell; going to court and telling a story about someone who had done something bad to you, but M did not have a story to tell. The most common method was to scare people, making them think you were going to hurt them unless they gave you what you wanted, but M was afraid to scare people. Her despair increased. She could not stop her desire, nor could she tell the difference between desire and necessity.

One day M was standing on the steps of the bank when a woman tried to hurry past. This happened all the time. Without thinking, M shouted, "Hey!" Her voice cracked but the woman looked up and, miraculously, reached into her purse and dumped some change into M's outstretched hand. M was exhausted from the experience. She retreated to her home to wait for dark and more TV.

The next morning M was on the steps with information she had learned just the night before: how to narrow your eyes and pull your lips back to show your teeth, in order to frighten people. Her new skills worked several times but many people still scurried past, and some who used to give her money now edged away.

That afternoon as M was walking down by the river, she saw something glint in the pale weeds. Watching TV had sharpened her eyesight. It was a gun. She picked it up and scuttled home. She did not know, but I did, that it was a beautiful, well-oiled Sig Sauer semi-automatic forty-five.

The gun changed everything. Suddenly TV had a vast amount to teach her. Over and over it showed her how to carry a gun, how to aim it, how to fire. She practiced along with the television. She understood: a gun was the best hope for achieving happiness.

She learned that a gun is typically used at night in a nearly deserted location. So one night she walked over to the theater district and waited nervously for the last of the plays to end. The audience poured into the street. Moments later the crowd thinned. When only one person was left, M came up to her and pointed the gun. Wordlessly, the woman handed over her purse. M, as she had been trained, found the money, stuffed it into her pocket, and threw the purse on the sidewalk.

M was overcome by her success and went home to contemplate her new-found power and wealth. She had almost fifty dollars. Although TV had been telling her what to do with money, now that she had it, she couldn't remember what she wanted. She searched the channels: here was a set of knives, here was a new cereal, here was some jewelry. She fell asleep, her head swimming.

When she woke up the next morning she had come to a decision. She walked to the bank and, for the first time, climbed to the top of the steps and went through one of the huge bronze doors. She blinked at the beauty of the columns reaching upward to the vaulted ceiling. After speaking to the guard, she was escorted into a polished wooden corral to see a bank officer. She emerged with a savings book.

The occupation of begging had come to an end. She went back to her house. She felt a desire to turn on her television. She was braver now; she let herself be enveloped in the richness of daytime and evening TV.

From that day on she rested and watched TV during the day; at night she traveled to various parts of the city where there were late-night bookstalls, restaurants, and theaters. She grew capable of two—sometimes even three—holdups per night. Her bank account grew steadily.

Last night around midnight M was waiting in a deserted street outside an expensive restaurant. A woman came out, weaving with intoxication. M walked up to her and quietly pulled out her gun. The woman pushed past her and staggered up the street.

"Hey!" M said softly.

The woman did not turn around or change her pace. M followed her. The woman went into an alley. A few feet away was a parked car.

The woman was trying to get her car key into the lock. M was behind her.

"Hey, your money!"

The woman turned and lurched—or fell—toward the gun.

M pulled the trigger and several shots exploded. The force of the blast threw her backwards and onto the ground; the gun flew out of her hand. Certain she had shot herself, she waited breathlessly for pain.

When it didn't come, she got up. She went over to the woman, who was lying in blood. M stumbled on the gun, picked it up, and ran.

I saw everything.

M walked around the city for a long time and finally came home. She has been up with the television on for the past few hours. What will she do? I cannot bear to lose her. I dare not interfere. Perhaps everything will be alright. Perhaps things can go on as before.

A Necessary *Hijrah*

IN THE *ERG* EVERY WANDERER has a means of survival: trader in salt, camel guide, thief. Sheherezade crossed the desert alone like a scuttling beetle. She went into the villages and told her stories in exchange for the necessities of the nomad's life she loved.

She was always mindful of the desert's demand for humility and surrender. She studied the forms of the harsh world and knew them well: shades and textures of sand, gravel veins, slopes, outcroppings, scents, stars, winds. She had never gone astray.

Then, somehow, she was lost. At first she was untroubled. She would discover a familiar landmark. At the southern horizon she saw a promontory and set her course toward it. The day grew hotter; mirages shimmered in and out of sight. Night came. She continued under the stars' familiar guidance. The next day and into the next night she went on. Her supplies were exhausted and so was she. She rested briefly, then started again before dawn.

As the day heated up the mirages returned. There was one that at first seemed no different from the rest. It disappeared—but was it behind a dune?—then returned, more distinct than before. Could it be a real place of life and water? She hesitated. Pursuing this mystery would take her off her course. She looked at the unbroken bleakness ahead. She knew she was in danger of perishing, whichever choice she made.

Mistrusting her impulse, she nonetheless turned and proceeded toward the beckoning vision. It disappeared and her heart sank. There it was again! Perhaps it was her imagination, but it seemed nearer still.

Without warning, a sword of darkness slashed down from the sky, laying waste to the mirage. She continued her approach and saw that the blade was a small windstorm, chasing itself in a dervish dance. Suddenly it stopped, revealing the stellated green of palms. In spite of hunger, thirst, and weariness, she ran toward it.

She was in a tiny oasis with a clear pool of water and abundant dates. She drank deeply, then ate. She pitched her tent and fell asleep. When she awakened near sunset, the sand was brilliant orange, the sky even more vivid: a wedge of purple moving across yellow and red, dragging a spangle of stars.

There was no evidence of former visitors to the oasis. It was as if she were inhabiting a mirage, so perfect and unlikely was her little paradise. She feasted on dates, lit a small fire, and made tea. Completely relaxed, she sat awhile beside the water, then slept soundly. Day after day she rested and revived. She sang, danced, told stories to the palms that bent their heads in grave attention. For the first time she was tempted to give up her nomadic ways, to take up the settled life she had always disdained.

One day a strong wind sprang up, spreading a fine grit of sand in the air, turning the blue sky red. The force increased: the sand jabbed at her, the sky turned leaden gray. Collecting dates and filling her water pouches, she retreated to her tent.

The wind intensified again. Sand came into her tent through every pore. She heard the palms rending and groaning outside. The tent collapsed. She wrapped herself tightly in it and waited for the gale to pass. She lost track of time while the storm prowled outside, biting and slashing at her skin of shelter.

The wind was unabated but she could not bear to lie still any longer. She unrolled herself from the tent and wound her scarf around her face. The tent whipped her and dragged her. She held on, sightless in the tumult. Then slowly, slowly, fold by fold, she at last managed to compress the frenzied canopy into a small bundle. She tied it to her body with the cord of her robe. Then she rooted in the sand, a blind creature, and found the rest of her supplies, which she lashed to herself as well. It was impossible to stand up; she fled by inching along on the ground, clawing at the flying sand, wondering if she would be buried alive.

The turbulence stopped. She was on her belly in burning sand. She stood and unwrapped her face. The desert stretched ahead, vast and unperturbed beneath a clear sky.

She turned and looked back. The snake of wind continued to spin, the oasis in its throat and vanished. She wept with relief and regret. In the hot air her tears dried halfway down her cheeks.

She turned again and gazed upon the promontory that was her guide. In sorrow she continued south.

The Monument

IN THE CAPITAL THERE WAS A MONUMENT, a small stone building with friezed walls and heavy iron gates. For many years the gates had been chained shut by order of the regime.

Growing up, N dreamed of the monument. What could be inside? Her heart smoldered with desire and resentment. Later she managed to obtain a room with a window that looked out onto her dream. She joined the resistance. Someday they would succeed in opening the monument.

Revolution came: there was bitter fighting and the old regime fell. A huge crowd was surging toward the monument, loudly singing a song of triumph.

N was in the throng. Her heart was overflowing with joy. She looked up at the sky and her voice flew from her throat like an uncaged bird.

Some people were carrying sledge hammers and axes. Arriving at the monument gates, they smashed at the chains, which withstood the blows at first and then gave way. The gates were flung open.

N jostled and pushed until she was in the front. No one tried to stop her; the mob seemed to sense her greater urgency. "At last," she thought, "at last."

She was standing on the threshold. She felt the out-flowing air on her face; it was cold and smelled of old stone and hermetic darkness.

Her body seemed to turn to granite. She stood like a boulder in a river while the crowd flowed around her. Then she turned and struggled against the current. The crowd parted as best it could to let her pass. She forced her way across the street to her building and ran up the stairs to her room. Without taking off her shoes, she flung herself into bed. She fell into a troubled sleep.

The next morning she was like a shard that she had once taken from the petrified forest—something once alive, now mineralized. She lay still the whole day. And the next. The third day she got up, put food into her mouth, chewed and swallowed it, and returned to bed.

She felt inert and confused. She felt like crying but no tears came. She saw herself in the throng at the monument, getting nearer and nearer, then finally going inside. At that moment her mind went blank and she fell asleep.

She woke up with a new thought: whatever was within the monument, it could never fulfill a lifetime of longing. She went back to sleeping the days away.

She was awake and the turmoil was gone. She was resolved: she would never go inside the monument. She arose and began her life again.

She was happier than she had ever been. Yearning unfulfilled was an unexpected source of contentment. After a meal, instead of a sweet, she would imagine it. Sometimes she would buy one and put it in front of her, feel her desire, and not take a bite. She would bring it closer and closer to her mouth and still she would not taste it. She felt unassailable, strong and complete.

Fighting broke out, the new government fell, the old one returned to power.

N rejoined the resistance. Once again her dream was of liberating the monument, knowing that when the battle was won, when the chains were broken and the gates were opened, she would stand outside in victorious longing.

The Sleeve

THE MAGICIAN OF THE PRINCIPALITY—who had come to be known as the Great Magician, or the Great One—was not only revered for her sorcerer's gifts, she was beloved for her wisdom and goodwill. Time passed and she grew so old a new Principal Magician needed to be found.

Word went out across the land: all magicians were invited to perform in a contest. The winner, chosen by popular acclaim, would become the next Principal Magician. There were no restrictions: each entrant might perform any conjuration and use any props or assistants.

In a village tavern two friends were discussing the upcoming tournament.

"I'll miss the Great One," sighed Dod the Woodcutter, sipping her beer.

"At least we'll see her assisting Vert at the contest," said Riv the Farrier.

"Finally we get to see that apprentice. She should be astounding after so much training."

Vert was alone in the Principal Magician's chamber, practicing for the contest. There was a soft knock at the door. It was, as she expected, the Great Magician.

"How is your preparation coming along?" asked her teacher.

"Very well."

"As I have said before, I would be pleased to assist you at the competition."

"I'd prefer to be alone on the stage."

"Why is that?"

"It's obvious, isn't it? I've been in your shadow for a long time. If I'm to be considered for Principal Magician, I need to be judged on my own merit."

"I will do as you wish. But everyone is ready to appreciate you for yourself, whether I am on the stage or not."

"I know that is how you see matters. I don't think you realize how adored you are. For the people, you are magic itself."

"I hope you are mistaken. I hope that people don't confuse me with the art."

"I think you are somewhat blind about this."

The woodcutter and the farrier were at the tavern the following evening.

"Did you hear?" asked Riv. "Vert is going to perform alone."

"I heard. How strange," said Dod.

"Maybe she has no need of the Great One."

The Sleeve

"How could that be?"

"Maybe she has surpassed her teacher."

It was a bright, still afternoon. A stage had been set up in a harvested hay meadow to accommodate a huge crowd. Everyone was sitting on the stubbly ground, eating, drinking, and chattering with anticipation.

With a fanfare of trumpets the contest began. Some aspirants were promising, some amusing, some merely impetuous. The throng was in a joyful mood, ready to appreciate any effort.

It was down to the last two contestants: Priot, long considered second in skill to the Great Magician; and Vert, the mysterious apprentice.

Priot climbed onto the stage with three assistants. Everyone had seen her countless times. Though proficient, there was something about her that had always troubled the populace. Something about her art seemed tainted, not entirely forthright.

At that time, pulling objects from a sleeve was at the height of its popularity. The Great One was the ultimate master of this magic, able to produce a whole barnyard of animals one after the other.

When it came time for Priot's finale, she chanted awhile, waved her wide sleeve, and produced a small goat. The crowd cheered. This was the best she had ever done. On prior occasions she had only managed various birds. But there was still something vaguely untrustworthy about the presentation.

It was time for Vert. As she walked onto the stage, the crowd drew in its breath and became still. Her robe had wide sleeves that trailed behind her. What wonders would spring forth?

Vert's performance went well. She ran through the introductory conjurations with ease. The midpart of the show was also competent and entertaining. But the finale was what the multitude was waiting for.

The apprentice spoke her incantation and flourished her sleeve. Out came a horse. The onlookers let out a wild cheer. Already Priot's goat was surpassed! What would be next?

Every eye was on the great sleeve.

Could it be that Vert was gathering up her props and leading the horse off the stage? The crowd turned silent. Was that all? Was this what they had been looking forward to for so long?

When it was clear that her performance was over, a few hands clapped out faint applause. Disappointment filled the air. Just a horse?

The spectators began to disperse, muttering to themselves and each other. Some say they saw the

Great Magician, who had been standing at the back of the crowd, walking away, looking down at the ground and shaking her head.

Everyone was upset. Why had Vert prevented the Great One from assisting her? Why had she deprived them of seeing their cherished Great Magician one last time? It could only be that the apprentice was full of pride and had not wished to share the stage. She had wanted to take all the acclaim for herself. Hadn't the Great One always said that sorcery was a gift, that though it gave the practitioner great power, it was the magic, not the magician, which was important?

From that day, a gloom settled over the land. Priot became Principal Magician but no one went to see her. No one spoke of it—the truth was too terrible to say—but magic, it seemed, had disappeared, perhaps forever.

Green Camp

WE SHUFFLED INTO THE ASSEMBLY ROOM, wondering what new injustice awaited us, what gnawing away at the tiny freedom still left to us. The Super takes such pleasure in our helpless anger, she calls these assemblies as often as possible. We slouched into our seats, determined to appear indifferent.

At the podium the Super, standing at stiff attention, looked almost unhappy. "As you may remember, there were several unfortunate deaths here last year." Her voice did not have its accustomed lilt; we could not suppress a thrill of expectation.

"The health board," she went on, "has completed its investigation of the matter. It has determined that the cause was, in part, due to the air quality, which is the poorest of any in our system. You are all at risk for lung disease. In terms of a remedy, expense is, of course, a factor. Rather than overhauling the ventilation system or building a new prison," she gave a short laugh, "a less costly solution has been reached." We watched her through seemingly impassive eyes.

"It was argued in the legislature that this plan was not suitable for prisoners, but, in the end, the modest budget of the proposal prevailed. Not far from here is an old camp that was once used by patients from the mental hospital. One week per year you will be sent there. This is not for enjoyment. It is purely to establish a minimum health standard. Dismissed." She marched off, her jaw grinding with displeasure.

Back in our cells we discussed the plan. "I never saw the Super look so miserable."

"That's got to be good news."

"If it's something good, they'll find a way to screw it up."

But hope glimmered in spite of our resolve to never hope for anything.

A few weeks later, in fierce heat, we were packed into ancient buses. We were hostile and crude, as usual. For self-preservation any eagerness had to be contravened.

We turned off the highway and lurched down an almost impenetrable road. Branches scraped and whined against the sides of the buses, weeds the size of small trees grew in the way. We came to what might once have been a clearing; now it was completely overgrown. Here and there were crumbling cinderblock structures.

We climbed down from the buses, already struck

by the bittersweet smell of plant life, the harsh buzzing of insects.

"Take these gloves and start pulling up brush. You and you, take these shovels. You're gonna dig some outhouses." The guards stood back and watched us, rifles at the ready.

We moved slowly, in the languorous rhythms of heat and prison culture. At night we slept on the ground, molested by insects. Later some new tasks were added: repairing the cinderblock buildings, smoothing fresh gravel on the paths we uncovered.

Then the week was over. There had been no respite, no activity except for the grueling labor of our sore, unschooled muscles. With some relief we thought of the indolence awaiting us in our cells.

When we returned, prison had never looked so dark, the air had never seemed so foul. The week at Green Camp was already fading into a moment of bright irrelevance.

Even in prison a year goes by; it was time for camp again. We could not quell a surge of anticipation—for a deep breath of clean air, for green, for sunlight. This time when we rode the buses, though our harsh banter was unchanged, we stole quick, hungry glances out the windows.

Green Camp

The camp was as we had left it. Weeds had sprung back and we were set to clearing and repairs. We were marshaled into an area that had once been a huge garden. Day after day we toiled, removing its wild overgrowth.

As we worked, something unbidden and unwise entered our hearts: we could not help but feel the beauty of the camp, could not resist falling in love. This time, when we left we carried a weight of regret. On the bus ride back we were exceptionally raucous, fending off the sorrow of parting with our only tool.

During the following year, though the incidence of disease was lower, there was an increase in rioting and suicide attempts. Green Camp, while healing one ill, had unleashed a far more dangerous malady, something all prisoners must guard against: heartache. After only two sojourns in camp, a reversal had taken place in our lives: camp had become our reality, our home; prison was the intermittent hell of exile.

We were on the bus to camp for the third time. We dissembled that we did not care but our hearts were bursting. When we got to camp we moved in a daze of love. We feasted on the light, the flutter of leaves and insect wings, the scents of broken stems and earth, the space around us, the exquisite air.

We worked without ceasing. Most of the time we were in the garden. We planted row upon row of crops that might possibly survive a year of neglect: Jerusalem artichokes, scarlet runner beans, garlic, parsley, chives, oregano. Bending over the soil, dirty to the elbows, we were happy and at peace.

Parting was a bit less painful this time. We were beginning to understand the patience and endurance required of love. We allowed ourselves the luxury of longing, for separation was temporary. Thoughts of camp sustained us through the year.

The next year we were amazed to see that a portion of all our crops had lived through their ordeal. We gathered them. We held them in our arms like infants, relishing their beauty and fragrance, the wonder of connection to this green world.

There were terrible rains and floods that winter. Buried in our cells, we scarcely noticed. But we worried for our camp, alone and unprotected in the storms.

We shuffled into another assembly. The Super was smiling as she mounted the podium. "I have some bad news about the camp," she announced triumphantly.

She could not have said anything more calculated to devastate us. We felt a terrible dread, as if friends and lovers had died and we had received our sentences, all on the same day. Outwardly we gave no sign of our anguish.

Her smile broadened. "There has been flooding all over the region. Everything in the camp is gone—buildings, trees, and the garden. All that's left is mud. We will be skipping Green Camp next year."

We held our breath.

"Then we will have to start over from scratch."

For once the Super had misjudged us. She was grinning as if she had dealt a death blow. All we could feel was relief. Two years. That could be done. And if we had to start over, that could be done, too. What were these tiny problems in the face of so great a reprieve? Our love was spared, our lives were saved.

Tears sprang to our eyes. No one moved to brush them away. It was never safe to show we cared.

The Foreign Woman

THE FOREIGN WOMAN WAS WALKING along the main street of the city. An old woman who was watching her had never seen such rudeness: this tall woman was walking right down the center of the crowded sidewalk, quickly, taking great strides, making way for no one, holding her head high, and seeming not to notice all the mistakes she was making.

"Terrible, terrible," said the old woman under her breath.

The next day she saw the foreigner again. It was the same as before: the racing woman seemed ignorant of the rules for keeping the head lowered, slowing down, moving out of the way. Others, too, glanced at the outsider with surprise and disapproval.

"Heh!" some of them shouted.

As the old woman looked on, a frail ancient woman was almost knocked over as the foreign woman sped by. "It might have been me," thought the old woman. She was as aggrieved as if she were the one who had nearly been dashed to the sidewalk, and without a flicker of apology.

The old woman could not stop thinking about the

matter. Every day she felt compelled to watch the tall foreigner as she passed by. It was always the same: the oblivious woman never stepped aside; others were forced to jump out of the way.

Hatred began to grow in the old woman's heart. She had difficulty sleeping. She knew that something must be done. A plan formed: she would lie in wait and then step out in front of the foreign woman. Just as she was about to be struck down, she would stab the foreigner with her curved knife. Even if she were caught, it was unlikely she would be punished. "Self-defense," they would say. "After all, the old woman was about to be trampled."

She stood at the edge of the sidewalk, grasping her knife inside her flowing sleeve. Here came the foreign face, high in the crowd.

Now!

The old woman, heart pounding, leapt forward.

Without slowing her pace, the foreign woman made a semicircle around the old woman and went on. The old woman went home, full of confusion. She could neither sleep nor eat.

The next day she stood at a different spot. Here came the face. Once again she lunged out. Again the foreigner made a swift half-circle and charged on.

"It was no accident," said the old woman to herself. "What can this mean?"

At home she paced and muttered all night. "Twice she has moved aside, for me and for no one else. Should I try a third time?"

Toward morning a change took place in the old woman's heart. She could not explain it, but she began to want to protect the stranger. "What if there are others hiding in wait with knives?" she kept thinking. "I must find out where she lives."

Someone was knocking on the foreign woman's door. "Who is it?" she called out.

"I must talk to you. It is very important."

The foreign woman opened the door. Who was this tiny old woman?

The old woman's words rushed out. "You do not know it but you are in danger. You need a handmaiden to protect you. I must do it."

The foreign woman began to close the door. "I am not looking for anyone," she said.

The old woman pushed hard against the door to keep it open. "I know this is true. I must be your handmaiden."

"I have no need for a handmaiden."

"I must do it. I feel it in my heart."

The two argued for awhile. Eventually the foreign woman gave in.

The old woman's knife is in her sleeve, at the ready in case of trouble. She cannot believe how fast she is moving, pulled along in the slipstream—no—the air is rushing full against her face as she moves up ahead, in front of the woman who steps aside for no one.

The Doorkeeper

THERE WERE MANY FINE APARTMENT buildings on the
wide boulevards of the city but the most elegant was
the E——. Its doorkeeper, Captane, was more imposing than all the rest. She was crisp and erect in her
maroon uniform with gold buttons down the front;
her maroon hat had a black leather visor. She had
been at the E—— for as long as anyone could remember. It was said that many tenants chose the building
because of her.

She learned the names of new residents the first
time they came through the wide front door. "Hello,
Ms. T——. Better button up, it's windy out there."
"Afternoon, Ms. M——, that's a beautiful scarf."

Captane quickly learned how each person liked
to be greeted, whether they preferred the door to be
opened well ahead of time or at the last moment, and
so forth. Should some special favor be needed,
Captane provided it with alacrity. Some tenants even
stopped by to talk to her about their troubles.

It was part of the culture of the E—— to be proud
of Captane. She was paid a good salary and everyone
gave her generous gifts at the holidays. She was treated

so well, and in return radiated such competence and goodwill, that each person was just a little bit happier and more considerate than at any of the other apartment buildings.

The inhabitants stayed on and grew old and so did Captane. Her hair turned gray and then white under her hat. Even so, her bearing, memory, and geniality remained impeccable.

It was time for Captane to retire. In the hallways and elevators there were secret meetings, whispers, and sly smiles. A surprise retirement party, a lavish one, was planned for the end of Captane's shift on her last day.

Retirement day was calm and sunny: no chasing of hats down the boulevard, no help with wet overcoats. In stealth the residents decorated the lounge and prepared for the party.

At the end of her shift, Captane, as she had always done, saluted the night guard who was coming on duty. The guard started to say something but at that moment a commotion started up in the lounge.

Captane walked over to see what was going on.

"Surprise! Surprise!"

It seemed the entire population of the E— was there, dressed up and smiling. Streamers crisscrossed the room, balloons clustered around the chandeliers, tables gleamed with white cloth. The smell of sizzling meat drifted from a long buffet, champagne corks popped. In one corner a small jazz combo began to play.

Captane was cajoled into leading the procession to the buffet. After heaping her plate, she was taken to a table with a huge bouquet at its center. She was joined by the E——'s owner, manager, and most distinguished clientele. Captane ate with gusto and accepted many refills of her champagne glass. People came by her table offering words of thanks and small wrapped gifts.

Management and guests beamed with pride and benevolence. How generous they were! How appreciative! A haze of well-being enveloped the room.

After dinner the owner stood. "Captane, we're sad to see you go. If I had my way, I'd keep you here another ten years. But it's only fair to allow you to retire, even though I fear the E—— will never be quite the same. We have a gift for you, a token of the gratitude we feel for your years of perfect service."

An envelope was stuffed into a pocket in Captane's jacket by the grinning manager seated next to her. Everyone cheered. After that, several residents stood up and told anecdotes of Captane's helpfulness.

Someone shouted, "Captane, how does it feel to be leaving?" Others in the crowd began chanting, "Speech! Speech!"

Captane had been eating and drinking throughout the testimonials. She stood and started to speak, then coughed and cleared her throat. The manager proffered a glass of water. Captane ignored it and picked up her champagne glass. She gulped down the contents amid more cheers.

A moment later, when she thrust her empty glass toward a passing waiter and nodded for more, realization coursed around the room: Captane was drunk! Still, the doorkeeper's back was as straight as ever.

"Someone asked," said Captane, "'How does it feel to be leaving?' I was raised that when someone asks you a question, it's like they opened a door. You have permission to walk through and tell the truth." She downed her glass of champagne and held it out again. The waiter poured it full.

"I watch you come and I watch you go, but I stay by the door. I don't come and I don't go. Maybe I could have, maybe it's my own fault. The truth is, I hated every minute of it. You all say how smart I am. I wasted it, my intelligence. I wasted my life. I can't begin to tell you how angry and terrible I feel."

She emptied her glass in one draught and walked out, erect but unsteady. The night guard saluted her as she reached the front door.

"You poor fool," said Captane.

Fulfillment

THE PROFESSOR WAS WORKING IN HER STUDY late one night when she heard a sharp knock on the door. A chill rushed across her back. "Who is it?" she called out.

"Do not fear," said a soothing voice. "Though it's true I am the Devil, I will not harm you." The Devil walked right through the door and entered the room. She had well-formed features but there was a subtle coldness about her which was vaguely frightening.

"Do you have any whiskey?" asked the Devil. The Professor did have a dusty old bottle high on a shelf. She got it down and poured a glass.

"Join me," said the Devil, in a soft voice that brooked no argument.

They drank. The effect on the Professor surprised her: she relaxed and yet remained alert.

"I have come to grant your every wish," said the Devil.

"Aha!" said the Professor. "I know how the story goes. You will give me everything but the price is my eternal soul. I am not going to make any deal with you."

"Since you are so astute," said the Devil, "I shall

extend an offer I have never made before. I will fulfill your every desire and I will not demand your soul in return."

"What is the trick?"

"There is none."

"You will take something else away, then?"

"I will not meddle in any other aspect of your life."

"There are no strings at all?"

"Not one. So come, tell me everything you have ever desired."

The Professor said nothing and sipped her whiskey. The Devil poured another glass. Eventually the Professor said, "I am not going to enter into a compact, but there is one thing I have always wished for."

"And what is that?" asked the Devil in her compelling voice.

"The only thing I have ever wanted is to be a great scholar. I dream of discovering some key piece of knowledge that has escaped everyone else. I would like to become known for this accomplishment and immortalized."

"It shall be done."

The Professor was silent, considering the matter.

"You must decide now. I have other visits I need to make tonight."

Suddenly the Professor said, "Yes, alright. Do I have to sign something?"

"No," said the Devil, and departed.

Over the ensuing years, the Professor, working steadfastly, was able to decipher an obscure text that had baffled scholars through the ages. One thing puzzled her: she experienced no pleasure in her efforts. She might as well have been pounding rocks into gravel, for all the satisfaction it brought. Nor did success bring any joy.

Then, when recognition began to come her way, it brought only the burdensome activities of posing for photographs, giving interviews, and receiving awards. Even when her place in history was assured, there was not one spark of enjoyment.

The Professor was old and dying. Her bed was made up in her study so that she could await death in her favorite place.

She was not surprised when the Devil walked into the room, asking, "How did you enjoy the fulfillment of your desire?"

"It was odd," said the Professor. "I succeeded completely yet I felt only duty and toil."

The Devil smiled. "Yes, there is the pleasure of

the quest for fulfillment, and there are the arduous chores that accompany success. A person must choose one course or the other."

"But deciphering the text took years. Why was I unable to be excited, especially as I was nearing the solution?"

"I confess my powers are limited. While I did my best to give you the experience of pursuing your cherished goal, the result, of course, was always assured. I have not been able to completely eliminate the effects of that."

"What if I had asked for both success and pleasure in the pursuit of it?"

The Devil laughed softly. "I could not have granted such a request."

"Ah, then there are things you cannot do. What else is beyond your power?"

"I shall not answer you. Already too much is known about me. It makes my task more and more difficult. But I still have a few tricks up my sleeve." The Devil bid the Professor goodbye.

The Professor lived one more day, during which a remarkable thing took place: she was suddenly filled with gratitude for the life she had lived, for its abiding toil. Then she died.

The Devil sensed that something had happened. She hastened to the Professor's study. The corpse was still warm; it had a smile of contentment on its face.

The Devil pursed her lips. Then she clenched her jaw and stomped around the room. "Too late," she muttered. "All my fine work has been spoiled."

I Am a Roman Slave

I WORK IN THE GALLEY SHIP OF A NOBLEWOMAN, rowing her across the sea. In secret I meet with others to plan the uprising: to overthrow the nobles and gain freedom. Our cause seems good, even glorious. I am prepared to give my life for it. Life is not long anyway.

At the meeting last night I spoke up. "I look forward to sitting on the shore and watching the light on the water when I am free."

I had assumed the rest of them felt as I did. I was told, "You must direct your thoughts to only two things: the injustice of our circumstances and the success of the revolution."

This freedom seems worthwhile but I shall not give up thinking about light, even if I am the only one and forbidden to speak of it.

I wonder why my love cannot be a part of freedom.

M—

M— was a beautiful town. Through its center coursed a river, lined on each side with lawns, gardens, and ancient shade trees. The citizens were proud of their town; tourists came to picnic and linger by the water.

M— was famous for polo. Stables and playing fields flourished. Everyone followed the matches with eager attention. Tournaments were held under multi-colored banners and celebrated with parades and festivals.

A horrible tragedy, an atrocity, took place in the town. News of it spread around the world. The event was so terrible that M— was associated with it forever afterward.

Time went on and the tragedy slipped into the past. The river still flowed, the parks endured, the stables and ponies remained.

At a council meeting a citizen stood and cleared her throat. "I think we should take down the banners at the polo fields."

Everyone agreed. They were relieved.

Later, the trees and parks were removed and replaced with dark paving stones.

M—— was gray and solemn. When travelers hastened through, they commented on how the appearance of the town fit its name. Polo was still played but it was unacceptable to mention it with any enthusiasm. The townspeople felt they deserved their punishment; many thought it should be even more severe.

A Model Farmer

WE FARM IN A WINDY LITTLE VALLEY. The soil is not the best and it is cold and rather bleak at all times. For this reason, perhaps, we are not a friendly lot. We are usually to be found with hunched shoulders and our collars up; a curt nod is our usual greeting.

"Did you see the notice?" asked a gruff comrade.

"No."

"Tacked to the meeting hall door. Something about a Model Farmers' Convention."

"What is it?"

"I don't know. We have to choose someone tonight."

That evening we packed into the hall. There were the usual disputes and mutterings: why should we bother, who should be picked, and so forth.

When the vote was taken, no one was surprised that it was Arva who was elected to go. She is the exception to the rest of us, a lamp of goodwill with a kind word for everyone. She performs little farming experiments which she records in her laboratory books. Sometimes she comes up with useful results. She is happy to impart them to anyone who is interested.

Arva stood and said, "Thank you for your confidence

in me. Whatever I learn I will bring back and share with you."

We were satisfied. She was our best offering. And she did not gloat about her victory, as others might have done.

The next morning Arva made her way to the train station. It was a long journey but she enjoyed looking out the window and meeting other passengers, several of whom were also delegates to the convention. Arriving, she and other Model Farmers were taken by bus to the convention hotel. The concierge came out to greet them.

"What a tall building!" said a Farmer.

The concierge bowed low. Then she straightened up and said, "Yes. And we have a roof garden where you may sit and enjoy the view, perhaps with an aperitif." The Model Farmers hastened to check in. It was almost time for the opening reception.

Arva entered the large room where the reception was being held, carrying a pen and notebook, ready to record useful suggestions.

Someone was at a lectern. "Welcome, Model Farmers. We have a great many events planned for you this week. Tonight and tomorrow you will be meeting each other and listening to lectures. After that we will begin touring, starting with the great wheat farm."

Most of the Farmers concentrated on eating and drinking as much as possible; some devoted themselves to socializing; Arva was one of the few who listened attentively to the speakers. Farming is going well and it will be going even better in the future—was the gist of every talk.

Arva thought to herself, "If this is all they are going to teach us, perhaps I should offer my help. I should have brought my laboratory books."

"What Lies Ahead," "New Approaches to Farm Management," "Toward a Bright Future": the lecturers next day droned on. During the breaks Arva met more Farmers. Even at the convention she stood out, due to her friendliness and sincerity.

After breakfast on the second morning the Model Farmers were packed into buses to visit the great wheat farm. "At last," thought Arva. "Now we will learn something." Soon the buses were moving through a blonde sea of wheat.

Arriving at the farm center, the group was dazzled by the tall silos, the massive combines, and the long metal sheds where various experiments were in progress. On the tour through the sheds, a guide explained the miniature models of irrigation systems, the prototypes for threshing machines, and the data on breeding experiments, new fertilizers, and pesticides. The Model Farmers were soon overwhelmed with information. They could not stop their minds from wandering.

Arva, however, continued to pay attention and a strange thing happened to her: she thought, "All this information is astonishing. I'm taking notes as fast as I can. I never dreamed so many experiments were under way, so many new ideas were being tested. What a fool I've been! My little farm, how pathetic it is. And how stupid of me not to have known that my experiments have already been done and surpassed here at the great wheat farm. I'm sure every idea I've ever had will be on display and improved upon."

She moved to the back of the group, full of terrible new feelings. A few of the other Farmers noticed that something was amiss and tried to catch her eye. She looked away.

At the lunch break in the huge dining hall, some of the Model Farmers asked her what was wrong. She was gripped with shame, thinking, "Look at these Farmers. They are excited by new ideas. I alone am corrupt, more concerned with my own success and failure than with the progress of farming. I always thought I was humble. It turns out I am as vain and petty as the worst of them. Worse."

Arva had always been honest. Now, for the first time, she lied. "As a matter of fact I think I'm getting sick." One of the workers was waved over and soon Arva was in the farm infirmary.

She lay on a bed in a bare room. She heard the buzz and whine of the combines as they made their way through the fields. She got up and looked out the window. Wheat fields stretched to the horizon. The sight was unbearable and she went back to bed. A nurse looked in and asked, "How are you feeling?" Arva turned away without a word.

It was late twilight when the Model Farmers gathered at the buses for the ride back to the hotel. Their arms were full of samples and brochures. Arva rejoined them.

"Are you feeling better?"

"Look, we have a bundle for you."

She took the bundle without comment. Seated on the bus, she closed her eyes and tried not to listen to the voices around her that buzzed and whined like combines. Unbearable. Everything unbearable.

The bus arrived at the hotel behind schedule and the Model Farmers rushed inside to dinner. Arva went to her room. A little while later she crept out and climbed the stairs to the deserted roof garden.

Something hit the awning over the hotel's front door with a loud *whump*. A guest standing underneath was startled by the noise. She ran to alert the concierge.

The concierge, along with a crowd of Model Farmers, rushed outside. A janitor climbed up a ladder to the awning. A moment later she called down, "There's someone up here. She's unconscious but her heart's still beating."

A few days later Arva awoke in a hospital. She felt pain in every limb. A nurse was peering down at her. "Time to start walking," she said.

Arva got up and shuffled down the hall behind a walker. "If only that damned awning hadn't been there," she thought. Several Model Farmers visited her. Everyone assumed the fall had been an accident. She pretended to listen to their chatter but she could barely stand it.

Word of Arva's misfortune got back to our valley and some of us took the train to see her. She was behind the walker looking pale and miserable.

"Hello, Arva."

"Hello."

"You must get well and hurry back to us. You are needed," we said, doing our best to cheer her.

In response her jaw clenched shut. "Too bad," she thought. "My mind is made up. I will finish what I started as soon as I can. But it is too difficult in a hospital, where one is watched all the time."

Late one night Arva returned to our valley. Everyone was at the train station, standing around awkwardly. As soon as she appeared, a shout went up. Someone made a speech to welcome back our Model Farmer.

"I'm very tired," she mumbled.

Back on her farm and alone at last, she lit a fire in the fireplace. She went over to the shelf that held her laboratory books. She opened the first one. She remembered when she had started it, full of excitement. How faithfully and neatly she had recorded each experiment. She threw the books into the fire.

Suddenly she was overcome with panic. She dashed outside and pumped water into a bucket, then ran back inside and threw the water onto the flames. Her books were charred and wet. The ink inside had run. Still, her notations were not completely ruined.

"How absurd I am," she said aloud. "First I try to destroy my books, now I try to save them. And they are as worthless as before." Nevertheless, she felt a speck of humor jump behind her eyes. "There is nothing for it but to go on with my ridiculous little projects. And why? For ambition. More than anything, I want to make a true discovery one day."

She went outside. The moon was half-protruding from a bank of clouds. She walked into her field.

"There was someone who experimented with pea plants," she said to herself. "Look what was accomplished. Then who can say what I may find?"

She paced excitedly up and down the rows of cultivation. "I will tell everyone the truth about what happened at the great wheat farm. I will tell everyone of my ambition. It will be embarrassing, but it is better than having such a thing be hidden."

Magic Dust

JAE THE FARMER WAS ALWAYS suspicious. In every interaction she was certain the other person had an ulterior motive and was lying. She was completely alone. Her neighbor was generous and devoted to good works. Jae wished she could start up a friendship but it was impossible, due to her wariness.

Jae thought to herself, "I will go to my grave without ever having a friend. What shall I do?" In desperation she made the journey to town to visit a famed magician.

"Help me if you can," said Jae, "though I doubt even you are capable of sincerity. I long for companionship but people are always deceiving me."

"I understand," said the magician. She handed the lonely farmer a small box, saying, "Inside is magic dust. When you throw it into the air, the first person it lands on, you will trust."

Jae took the box and started back to her farm. She planned to throw the dust on her neighbor at the first opportunity.

A little way out of town she was suddenly overtaken by a fierce windstorm. It was pulling up fences and bushes. It seized the box of magic dust from Jae's hands, flung it high into the air, and carried it away.

A gang of bandits was hiding in a thick grove of trees beside the road, waiting to waylay unsuspecting travelers. Suddenly a box dropped from the sky and fell on the leader's head. She was Hanje, a notorious and ruthless criminal. The box came open and something powdery spilled all over her.

"What the hell?" she shouted, brushing the powder off as best she could.

"Ha ha ha!" laughed the gang.

"Quiet! I hear someone coming."

Jae was upset about the loss of her magic dust and the wasted trip to the magician. "I'm sure that magician tricked me somehow," she thought. She was anxious to get home after her ordeal. The road was heading into a grove of trees.

She heard a rustling sound.

The bandits leapt into the road in front of her. She gasped in surprise. But something about the leader seemed reassuring.

"Hand over your money," demanded Hanje, brandishing a weapon.

"Certainly," Jae replied.

The gang stared. "Odd," they muttered.

Jae offered what money she had. Hanje grabbed it and turned to her companions. "Let's go."

Jae waved and called out, "Goodbye."

Later the thieves were dividing up the day's plunder. They started talking about the peculiar woman in the grove. "I never saw anyone so lighthearted about giving up her money."

"Maybe we should see if she has anything else."

"Let's find out where she lives and rob her," said Hanje.

A few nights later the thieves broke into Jae's farmhouse. Jae was awakened by sounds in the dark; she began to scream.

The gang wanted to leave, but Hanje had an inspiration. She held a lantern next to her face and went into Jae's bedroom.

On seeing the familiar face, Jae calmed down and smiled. "It's you! Hello."

"You really are mad," said Hanje. The thieves took the silverware and a painting.

Jae called out, "Goodnight!"

"Crazy," declared the gang.

Over the ensuing days the bandits continued their discussion of the deranged woman. Did she have more valuables? Since she seemed friendly toward Hanje, perhaps the leader could cajole her into revealing anything she might have hidden.

Hanje knocked on Jae's door. Jae opened it and smiled broadly. "I was hoping you would visit me. Come in."

The two began to spend time together. Jae was delighted to at last have a friend. Hanje stole from her at every opportunity and tried to find out if she had anything else of value.

One day Jae said to the thief, "It's strange, but a few odds and ends of mine seem to be missing."

"I think I saw a suspicious-looking person making off with some of your things just a little while ago. If you wish, I will guard your house."

"Would you? I'll give you a key so you can come and go as you like."

Hanje added, "Sometimes thieves will go looking to see if you have anything hidden nearby. Should I watch for that, too?"

"How thoughtful you are. Let me show you where I buried a small chest in my pasture. It contains some jewels and a few gold coins. I'm so fortunate to have such a trustworthy friend."

Jae showed Hanje where the chest was buried. That very night the gang came by and dug it up.

There were still a few pieces of furniture left, so Hanje returned.

Meanwhile, people were talking about Jae. "She has become completely insane."

"Remember when she was so aloof and mistrustful? Now she has turned into a gullible fool."

Hanje, seeing that Jae would believe anything, told bigger and bigger lies. One day, just to find out what would happen, she said, "The sky is green."

Even Jae could see it was not true. "Hanje, I'm sorry to have to tell you this, but I think you are inclined to lie at times. It doesn't trouble me because I know you have a good heart."

Over and over the thief told lies. Jae serenely pointed them out. Then, inexplicably, Hanje began telling the truth. But only to Jae.

The Last Criminal

I ALMOST NEVER TAKE WALKS without a destination but I was restless. The woman from Yale wasn't due until ten and the house was clean, the danishes were set out, and I still had an hour to kill. My feet took me over by the cannery, to a neighborhood with some small run-down houses. I was glancing in the picture windows when I saw a dining room tableful of kids. From the back, I saw a brown-haired kid suddenly reach over and punch a younger kid on the arm, hard. A few moments later the same brown-haired kid took some food off the other's plate. This was impossible. Yet I saw it as clearly as if it were the movies, framed by the picture window. I walked home in a state of agitation.

I made a pot of coffee and was on my first cup when the doorbell rang. It was the Bundt woman from Yale. She was carrying a beautiful briefcase that looked older than she did. I sat her down at the kitchen table with the coffee and danishes. She didn't touch anything. Right away she opened the briefcase and pulled out a stack of papers.

"As I mentioned in my letter," she said, "we, the

Historical Criminology Department, are pleased to offer you an honorary doctorate in recognition of your services to the field."

For a second I thought I wasn't hearing her correctly, but I have perfect hearing. Services to the field? I felt like I was being offered a reward by the police, like I was a stool pigeon or something. I was angry but I didn't know it right away. I just got that light-headed, sinking feeling I get sometimes. I was telling myself, "Look, this poor chump is just a representative. Don't take it out on her." Mostly I was blaming myself.

"What?" I said.

Bundt said, "You have contributed a great deal to the understanding of the nature and practice of crime. Universities sometimes reward outstanding contributors with honorary degrees." She was sitting there beaming steadily at me with her shoulders back, obviously expecting me to be pleased.

When I didn't smile or say anything, her face drooped a little. Maybe she thought I was unhappy about there being no money that came along with the deal, because she added, "Yale has the most extensive archives of historical criminology in the world. On occasion we might confer with you about the authenticity of some of our documents. If so, you would be paid a consultant fee."

I was sunk halfway through the floor and breathing hard. I said quietly, "Well, I'd like to think it over."

Bundt seemed to sense my tension. She stood up quickly. "I'll just leave the materials with you for your perusal. If you have any questions, please don't hesitate to contact us." Then she beat it.

I sat there like a dope. Like I had been hit with a sock of sand. Things had gone too far. Don't ask me why, but the waxworks museum popped into my mind: that figure of me crouched down with my ear against a safe, my fingers on the dial, a bluish-gray gun stuck into the waistband at the back of my skirt. But even when I was younger, I didn't have the ruthlessness about the lips they had given me. The waxworks was an emblem of what had happened. I was frozen in a pose for the entertainment of others. Reporters were always cycling through asking the same questions: how many safes did you crack? How many people did you shoot? Tell us about your narrow escapes. How many times did you work with so-and-so?—referring to one or another of the notorious criminals of my day.

It all began—or began to accelerate—with the

Newark Park deal. I signed a contract that allowed them to use my name and face in a new ride called the Getaway. Next they wanted me to come for the grand opening. I was strapped into the first car of the thing with a kid next to me and we flew off into the dark. Bullets sizzled past and sirens blared. The ride was nothing like a real getaway; it was louder, more jolting, more colorful. But it was enjoyable and, judging from the screams, scary enough. The problem was afterwards: coming out into the sunlight and having to talk to the reporters.

Suddenly I was someone else who was supposed to be all for kids having a good time, supposed to grin and be a nice, harmless person. It was an erosion. Next came the cereal, the doll, the game, the tee-shirt. The money was good and it was easy, except my soul was getting eaten away bit by bit and I wasn't even paying attention.

I started having dizzy spells. Light bothered me. They wanted appearances doing things like judging a teenage wrestling championship at a beach in LA in absolutely blinding sunshine. I'm a night person. It was crazy.

I was asked to be on a telethon for kids who were victims of things like auto accidents and falling out of trees. I was supposed to be reassuring and folksy. They kept telling me I was doing a great job and the money was rolling in. I felt so woozy I thought I was going to fall through the stage.

After that I put my foot down: no more appearances or products or interviews. But it was too late.

All the information I had given the press and everyone else over the years hadn't helped anyone understand me or my vanished breed. The more I talked, the worse it got. They wanted to make it so that crime was an amusing bit of history. I never should have opened my mouth. I never should have done the Getaway and the teenage wrestling and the telethon and the waxworks and all the rest. The world had done everything to bury me alive, to turn me into something historical even as I sat eating a danish across the table.

I poured myself another cup of coffee. It was embarrassing to admit, but I was proud of being the Last Criminal. I would rather be the last one than have to share the limelight with someone else. Plus, if I distorted the truth of my life, exaggerated a bit, there was no one to correct me. The price of distortion was the dizziness and anger; it would probably kill me. Then there would be no

Last Criminal, there would be no criminal at all.

Once there were so many of us. Once it was a network that embraced the earth, an interwoven lattice. It was called the underworld but it was more like hovering above, an overworld. Everyone was committed; every waking moment renewed our awareness of belonging to something different. We had to trust each other to a much greater degree than did those below. To float above, we had to keep the lattice strong. That's why squealing was such an unforgivable act: when one of us sank, a portion of the lattice could be dragged down and torn apart. There would be a pulsing wave of fear, then the task would begin—of removing the damaged edges and weaving the threads of loyalty back together.

It was a glorious time. I'd wake up in those late afternoons, thrilled at the adventure that lay ahead, almost breathless from my good fortune. And to think I might have turned out to be a chump. Of course there was always risk: doing something stupid, getting caught. But part of the creed was that if you were smart enough you could always escape. There were legends about it, people who pulled off hundreds, even thousands, of jobs and got away. My heart always pounded; it heightened my intelligence and skill. I was never caught. After awhile they told stories about me, too, during those long stretches of waiting and those victory celebrations when some big take was divided up.

There seemed to be the perfect number of us: not so many we overran each other's territories, nor so few that things could not be done properly; not so many we became commonplace, nor so few we were merely eccentric; not so many the lattice fell to earth, nor so few it floated away, a gossamer dream. Old members died or retired, others moved up in rank, beginners eagerly joined. For a long time it was a perfect life. Although we used words like "job" and "work," it was a joke. Work was, perhaps, what beginners did: standing in the rain and cold as look-outs, carrying tools, doing errands. But it was never work, because the money came from something like a sports event, like big game hunting. Below us the chumps were doing routine and deadening things; we alone were blessed with endless excitement.

Some of us found our niches and became masters of a craft. Mine was opening safes. I got into it by accident. Early on I was carrying tools for a master cracker. She didn't show for a job one night so I did what I had seen her do many times: I placed my fingers on the safe's dial and slowly twisted it, listening for clicks. I cracked it the very first time. I had a gift. After awhile I switched to my left hand and ear and got even better. Safes were like mysterious metal animals to me; I could hear their soft heartbeats. Later, when there were opportunities to move into administration, I chose to remain where I was. I was happy. Administration had its own risks. You made more money but you had more worries. That's where the territory problems came up; that's where the lattice itself tried to strangle you at times. Those with a craft were valued. We had a kind of immunity and tremendous pride.

Then something began to change in the overworld. The old-timers retired earlier; the movement upwards was more rapid but fewer recruits were joining. There was a sense of discouragement. The lattice started dissolving until one day it was gone. There were only local groups and then just a few people working together and then loners again.

I am no expert on the chump world but I look at the papers and I saw changes going on there, too. For some reason people started obeying the laws. They drove at the speed limit, returned lost wallets, stopped cheating on their taxes. Then they even stopped playing poker and practical jokes. Crime became a thing of the past—alluring and unfathomable.

Friends died one after the other. They smoked too much, drank too many highballs, ate too much. They grew careless about everything.

The hardest thing is the loneliness. I can't cross over into the chump world; there's no one in it I remotely respect. When I go near it I feel like I'm starting to spin, like I'm turning into a giant drill and boring down through the floor.

Thirteen years ago when Georgiana Gagney died, I was left alone. Gagney never worked with me; she was a forger and we didn't move in the same circles, but we were the last two. Because of that we made each other's acquaintance. We'd get together in the evening, sit outside on deck chairs, and watch the stars rise and fall. At first we tried to talk about old times but our hearts weren't in it. Mostly we were silent, sharing the impossibility of conversation. Neither of us knew what to make of the world we had lost.

When Gagney died the Last Criminal idea started up. There hadn't been any Last Two Criminals. After Gagney died, it was open season. It was as if they had finally cornered the wild animal and could do whatever they wanted with it. They were right, almost.

Which brings me to the Yale incident. The truth is, when I got the letter, I thought it had something to do with my self-education program. I've always read a lot, including dictionaries and grammar books, to improve myself. Like a dope I thought maybe they were going to honor me for that. Historical criminality? Who are they trying to kid?

I had enough thinking for one day. I was tired and went to bed. I dreamed I was in a field, a bit like my old elementary school. Kids were throwing dirt clods at me and calling me names. There was a safe next to me. I got down and started working on it. There was so much noise I couldn't hear the clicks. I felt panicky. I hugged the safe—just put my arms around it like it was my last friend in the world, like I was reassuring it I still cared.

I woke up thinking maybe I'd pull a job of some kind. There were several problems: I didn't feel like travelling; I would have to do it by myself, which was never my style; if money turned up missing, everyone would immediately think of me. But who would catch me? The police didn't arrest people anymore, they just acted helpful and directed traffic. There were no courts, no prisons. Maybe they would put me in the jail at Knott's Berry Farm. "Yes, folks, see a live criminal serving time. Feedings at 7, noon, and 5 p.m." Prison. So much is gone. So much is lost.

I fell asleep again. I dreamed I was in the joint. I was sentenced to live forever and never get out. The cell turned into my house. Barricades were being built around it, thicker and thicker, until I could barely hear the hammers as new layers of impenetrability were added. My house was empty but there was a kitchen table with a knife on it. I thought, "If I cut my heart out and look at it while I'm still alive, my sentence will end."

When I woke up again it was only mid-afternoon. I put on a semi-disguise, floppy-brimmed hat and sunglasses, and went out. There were several banks nearby; one had a huge banner inviting everyone in for free food.

Inside, it was cheerful, not too big. There was glass everywhere and philodendrons. Some security cameras were pointing every which way and falling off their brackets. There was no guard, not even a buzzer system. The big safe looked like a family member, I knew it so well. I had some cheese cubes and fruit salad and opened up an account.

The woman who took my information stared at me. "Excuse me, but aren't you the Last Criminal?"

Oh, what the hell. "Yeah."

She looked pleased with her discovery and made a little joke. "This is quite a turnaround, you putting money *into* a bank."

I started to get that downward-spinning feeling but I held on. It came down to this: the only interesting part of a job would be to see what they did to me. It all felt vaguely familiar but also so unfamiliar I could have been in one of my strange dreams. Why did they even have banks anymore?

She called over the assistant manager, Ms. Fankie, who was terribly polite and introduced me to the staff. Everybody wanted to shake hands and say cute things. Afterwards Fankie followed me out to the sidewalk.

When we were alone she said, "You're not going to believe this, I'm not sure I do. But I don't know where else to turn."

"What is it?" I asked, wondering what could possibly be eating her.

"I have a cousin. She runs a corner store over near the cannery. Last week she called me, all upset. She said she could have sworn a child came into the store with two friends and stole a can of soda. The friends bought snacks but the child didn't get anything. At the end of the day a can of soda was missing."

A jolt of foreboding made me shiver. I had managed to forget about the picture window incident but it came back in a flash. I felt uneasy—not the human drill feeling, more like a dream—like my mind was moving too fast for my body, my body turned into a shadow, the shadow disappeared. I kept thinking, "If I could only change how I'm looking at everything, I could be at peace, or at least get back to the familiar patterns that pass for peace."

"What do you want me to do?" I asked.

"Would you look into it for us? No one else would believe it for a second. But my cousin—"

"I'll think it over." I walked away fast. Everything about the day had been upsetting.

I wasn't sure I wanted to be there, but I was back in the neighborhood by the cannery. I found the corner store. Several groups of kids went into the store and came out sipping sodas and eating candy and chips. Then I saw, from the back, a group of three kids going in. One of them had brown hair that looked like the kid in the picture window. By the time I followed them into the store, the owner was leaning over the counter, fixing her eyes on them.

"So, what are your names?"

"Britt."

"Tami."

The brown-haired kid didn't say anything. Tami answered, "Monad."

"Okay," said the storekeeper. "Just make sure you remember to pay." The kids bought their stuff. On the way out, Monad took a swipe at Tami, a fairly hard punch on the shoulder. Tami acted like it didn't happen. As they walked off, Monad was grabbing chips out of Tami's bag.

I got that bad dream feeling again. I felt weak. I left the store and forced myself to follow the kids.

I was remembering my own childhood. My sisters and I were poor; the two aunts who raised us worked chump jobs in a factory. Back then I thought about going to college. But when a friend asked if I wanted to try something a little risky that might make some good money, I said sure. I flew into my new life like a bird flying up into the treetops and never looked back. I was a clean-cut kid before, and a clean-cut criminal afterwards, like most of the smart ones. I never picked fights or did stupid petty stuff.

Monad was a pint-sized version of a punk. But there weren't any more punks.

I followed the kids down the block. I wasn't surprised when Monad took off and went into the house

113

with the kids in the picture window. I came home, took a shower, and tried to go to sleep. That didn't work so I got up and started polishing my tools. My gun, too. Pulling a job seemed a waste of time but everything was ready to go. I kept thinking about the kid. Now Fankie's problem was eating me.

The next afternoon I waited outside the kid's house. Right on time the kid came bouncing along, eating a bag of potato chips. I had worked out a story but suddenly I just blurted out who I was.

The kid said, "So? What do you want?"

I said I wanted to talk.

The kid asked why.

"I don't know. I'm curious."

"Well I'm not curious about you."

I got an inspiration. "How about I buy you some chips, ice cream, whatever you want."

"Okay."

We went over to a diner and sat at a booth. I looked across the table and saw the kid's face for the first time. It was not what I expected. Her face was radiant and mysterious. The eyes behind a long veil of bangs were extraordinarily lively. I didn't know what to make of it. The kid had the face of an angel.

Monad ordered a milkshake, burger, and fries. I

waited awhile for her to eat. The food seemed to mellow her a bit.

I started off, "Tell me about yourself."

"What do you want to know?"

"You have a reputation for causing trouble."

"That's a lie."

"You mean you don't cause trouble?"

"No."

"What would you call it?"

"I do stuff."

"What kinds of stuff?"

"Did you see?"

"A couple of things."

"That's it."

"Grabbing chips, taking swipes at people, stealing soda?"

"Yeah. Cheat at school, cut school. Lie." The kid was warming up. There was a hint of a smile. It was beatific. "Yank hair. Scare my little sister."

Monad reminded me of people from my past, alright. There was something chilling about this kid.

"Why do you do it?"

The kid shrugged.

"Really. Why?"

She said matter-of-factly, "Because I want to and

115

I can." Then she went back to sucking on her milk-shake. It was gone and she was just making loud noises with the straw.

"Doesn't anybody try to stop you?"

"No. I keep on trying new things. I get more and more stuff, I hit people harder and harder. It's easy."

"You know who I am, right?"

"I'm not stupid." She sucked through her straw for awhile. "You got any equipment? You know, crime stuff? A gun maybe?"

My heart turned frosty. I was not going to give this unnatural kid any of my prize tools. "I think it's time to go," I said.

The kid took a final slurp and left.

I felt confused and sick and came home. There wasn't anything I wanted to do. Nothing about my life seemed remotely worthwhile. I got into bed with my clothes on, pulled the covers up around my chin, put a pillow over my eyes, and tried to sleep. Instead I cried like a baby. Then I dozed off.

I woke up after a lot of bad dreams, thinking, "It's over, it's all over." It didn't make sense but I felt tricked, like I was set up, way back. I resented every-one I ever knew. It was just a big scam and I was the mark. It was set up to look like I was this great safecracker, but all along I was being used, losing more and more. I couldn't remember ever feeling lower.

I cried some more and went back to sleep. I dreamed I died. I had a beautiful casket and lots of people were paying their respects. Then Monad showed up and everybody stopped paying attention to me and started fawning all over the kid, who was now a big shot.

I woke up again and got up. Sleep wasn't helping.

It was dark out, which was perfect for the plan. Just a sliver of moon giving almost no light. It didn't matter, I have bat vision. I was carrying my tools and my gun to make it feel realistic. It was kind of pathetic, like a former athlete going to the gym, just trying to keep in shape. That's all it was, keeping in shape. Something to do and something to prove to nobody but yourself.

I was walking toward the bank but something was missing. My heart was as quiet as if I were cutting my toenails. A job was supposed to raise your heart rate, not calm it down. I sat on a bench to try to think. Then I stood up and my feet went toward the kid's place. My heart rate was picking up a little.

I had come to a decision: ice the kid. I couldn't keep having those dreams. The way the kid was headed, she would be trying bigger and bigger stuff. Until the kid would be the big criminal and I would be history, meaning no longer history. I had worked too hard and lived too long to let some punk kid steal my legacy. I had never iced anyone in cold blood before. Self defense a couple of times. Never a kid. This would wake everybody up alright. No more telethons for me.

I went to the back door of the kid's house. I was starting to pick my way in when I realized the door wasn't even locked. Nobody locks their doors anymore. Everything is so screwed up. I went down the hall. In the dimness I could see the kid's door: "Monad" was written on it in letters a foot high. Inside, the kid was wrapped up in a dirty comforter. I put the gun next to her temple and gave a little nudge. She woke up fast.

"What do you want?" Cool as a cucumber.

"Let's go."

The kid slept in her clothes. She put on her shoes and preceded me down the hall. We headed over to the darkened cannery. We were in an alcove, about ten feet across and twenty feet deep, with the high walls of the cannery on three sides and the fourth side open to the weedy parking lot. I set the tool kit down on the ground. I was pointing the gun at the kid who was against the back wall. Still not a whimper.

We stood there awhile. For the first time in a long time my heart was going fast enough to clear my head. I kept the gun pointed and used the opportunity to think. What is this Last Criminal crap, anyway? This legacy crap? Contributions to the field, interviews, celebrity status. Pure chump crap. To make the chumps' sad little lives a bit more tolerable. What good had it ever done me? Just a lot of mistakes and humiliations I'd rather forget. My life was always about the dough and the excitement, period.

It felt good to be thinking straight. I looked over at the kid who was motionless as a statue but not giving off any fear. What to do about that? Cold blood seemed so damned—cold-blooded. I had to at least make it interesting.

"Okay, kid. We're going to have a little contest. Sort of like a duel only there's only one weapon. I'm going to set the gun down and walk back a ways. When I say 'go' we're both going to run for it. Whoever gets it can do whatever they want."

The kid didn't say anything.

"You got that, kid?"

"Yeah."

I set the gun down, the barrel pointing sideways, and backed up about twenty feet.

"Go."

We both scrambled. The kid was fast but my legs were twice as long. We got to the gun at the same time.

I gave the kid a shove and she went down on her back on top of the gun. She hauled off with a brutal kick that caught me on the shin. I bent down and gave the kid a wallop on the head. I was trying to roll her off the gun when she kicked again and got me on the ear and I went down this time. I sat down hard on the kid's middle. A second later the kid bit me on the hand. I pulled my hand away and banged the kid's head down on the pavement and held it there. I was sitting on one of the kid's hands and I grabbed the other one with my free hand and held it down on the ground. The kid was pinned. Neither of us could get to the gun: the kid was on it and I was on the kid. Nobody said a word; we were both breathing fast from pain and effort. Then the kid let loose with a huge wad of spit and caught me in the face. I went blind with fury.

That fury did something to me. It was like a white-hot fire that burned through everything. For the first time in ages I felt pure rage that wasn't all mixed up with guilt and anger at myself. I felt cleansed by the heat of it. Suddenly my heart went easy. I had the feeling of being up on the lattice, back where I belonged.

The kid started squirming. "Let me up."

"Just a minute. I've got to figure this out."

"Let me up."

"There's still the matter of the gun."

"I won it."

A few things still weren't quite clear in my brain. I sat awhile longer, holding the kid down. The kid was some fighter. She was wriggling like a canful of worms. She probably deserved something for that.

"Tell you what. I'm giving you the tools. But not the gun."

"But I won it."

"I don't know about that, but anyway, I changed my mind."

"That's not fair."

"Maybe, but that's it."

"I can't ever have the gun?"

The kid relaxed for a second and I jumped up, rolled her off the gun, and grabbed it. The kid lunged up after it but I held it high. The kid was fixing to take another kick. I saw it coming and stepped away. "Am I going to have to aim this at you again? Back off."

"It's mine. I won the contest. Or you want to fight some more?"

"Just listen for a second." Understanding finally lit up my mind. "You're not ready. A gun has to be earned."

"Do more bad stuff?"

"No. You want to be a criminal, be a smart one. Study, learn what it's all about. Get some self-control and some manners."

"Then can I have the gun?"

"We'll see."

"Okay." The kid picked up the tool kit and sauntered off.

I put the gun in my pocket and started walking home. I realized I was famished and headed for the diner instead. It was just beginning to get light. I always loved that after a job.

A Mirrorist

JEL, A MIRRORIST, WAS WALKING ALONG on the side-walk one afternoon. She saw a woman standing by the curb, whose face was contorted in horror and panic.

There was a time when Jel was unaware of her gift. Later she discovered that she took on the mannerisms of everyone she met—speech, gestures, facial expressions. It was automatic yet also deliberate: she would enter the other person and feel what they were feeling. In a sense, for at least a moment she *was* the other person. That person, on encountering the mirrorist, would have the sensation of being understood, though without knowing why. For Jel the experience was often painful. It was also fascinating. She could not help feeling proud of her special faculty and some degree of pity and disdain for those who did not possess it.

Actually, the woman on the curb was enjoying the afternoon. Her face had frozen into its nightmarish grimace as a result of repetition and habit. Primarily, it was from squinting. She saw the mirrorist coming toward her.

"What an awful expression she has on her face,"

thought the squinting woman. "It's such a shame to see a face so twisted up." She recalled that from time to time she had seen other people with the same strange look. "What could they have been so upset about?"

A short distance behind the mirrorist, a young girl was walking along. She was oblivious to everything around her, thinking about herself and her good fortune.

The woman by the curb looked past the mirrorist to the self-absorbed young girl. "What a difference," she thought. "Now *she* is a pleasure to look upon." She tried to maneuver her face into a smile for the cheerful girl. It was impossible; she only managed to look still more horror-stricken.

This caused Jel to experience a fresh burst of anguish.

A Shame and a Pity

THE HOT AIR BALLOONS WERE SAILING in the blue sky, dazzling in the high pure world. Though all were beautiful, there was one that was much larger and more magnificent than the rest. It sailed above the others like a blessing and a promise. The aeronauts called it the Great Balloon.

They were shouting across to each other, "Look at it up there, it lifts my heart just to see it."

"Perfection."

"I must have one like it someday."

The aerostats were so enchanting, no one ever thought to look at the people who kept them aloft. The pilots' voices, at least, gave the impression of contentment, even of indolence.

Jae, the creator of the Great Balloon, hung beneath it in a small basket. She was aching in every limb. Her body was down to the barest of sinews, so strenuously did she toil. In the basket was a grate, a supply of fuel, and a small bellows. Most of the time she pumped the bellows to keep the flame at a proper pitch; occasionally she hurriedly threw more fuel onto the grate. As a result, her vessel never faltered in its course.

Jae did not know if the other sailors were working so hard: she was too busy to look down. Sometimes she called out to learn how they were faring, but these queries coming from *that* balloon were treated lightly. The other pilots could not imagine anything amiss with the object they all aspired to. Though Jae was proud of her creation, the effort required for gliding in the sky, for the majesty and seeming ease of it, was close to unbearable.

On this perfect day the splendor of the sky, the beauty of her balloon, the admiring comments were not enough. Jae thought, "Perhaps I am weaker than everyone else. I cannot go on."

She put down the bellows and stopped throwing fuel onto the grate. All was well. Then she noticed a slight dimpling in the balloon's flawless skin. The craft sank until it was a little lower than the others.

She felt torn between exhaustion and an impulse to resume her efforts. If she would just pump the bellows she would rise again. But she did nothing. She heard shouts of disbelief and alarm.

"What is it? Are you alright?"

"How can this be happening?"

The balloon was elongating, its sides becoming furrowed like a drying fig.

The sailors began to discuss the situation.

"I've always thought there was something wrong with that balloon."

"It's too grand."

The Great Balloon lurched lower.

" . . . Must be her fault . . ."

" . . . Brilliant but unsound . . ."

" . . . A shame . . ."

" . . . A pity . . ."

Jae fell further and the words became indistinct. She remained motionless. She felt a surge of desire to survive the descent, but still she could not bring herself to act.

Below was a rocky outcropping.

Most of the envelope was hanging and limp, the weight of its material driving it downward. The final drop was swift. She landed on a narrow spike of rock; the balloon collapsed around her like a shroud.

Jae crawled out and looked up. The others were sailing on. Their voices grew fainter and fainter until it was completely quiet.

When she stood up, the rock was sharp on her bare feet. She began to climb down the crag. As for the pain in her feet, she welcomed it.

The Biographers

THE AUNTS WERE SCATTERED at small tables throughout the upstairs library. They were bent over their work, spines sharply curved like their gooseneck lamps. They wrote biographies of famous poets. You would recognize the books, beautiful volumes reflecting massive research and impeccable erudition.

Jieme, their only niece, was at a large table in the center of the room. The aunts had finally convinced her to take up the family trade; she had been at it for two weeks.

She tapped her pencil on the tabletop and let out a loud sigh. "I can't stand it." The aunts raised their heads in unison. "I can't stand another minute of this."

An aunt cleared her throat and said, "How is that possible? We gave you one of the most interesting poets who ever lived."

"I don't care about her. And I don't care about these horrible biographies."

"You'll get used to it," said another aunt.

Tap tap tap.

"What *do* you want to do, then?"

"I don't know." Tap tap.

"Quiet, please. I'm trying to concentrate."

Jieme broke her pencil in two and ran from the room. For several years an occasional postcard was the only word from her.

The oldest aunt died. Without much hope, a letter was sent to Jieme's last known address.

It was after midnight when the front doorbell started ringing. The remaining aunts roused each other and, like a flock of ghosts, descended the stairs. Of course it was Jieme.

They all mourned. Glowing obituaries appeared in the newspapers. Luminaries dropped by to pay their respects.

After a week had passed, the aunts gave a formal dinner. The biographers sat ranged around the table, hunched and stern. Their publisher, editor, and an acclaimed poet were there.

The publisher wiped her mouth and turned to Jieme. "So, when will I be seeing your first biography?"

Jieme drew a circle in the air with her fork. "Oh, you know."

"Soon, I hope. It's time for the next generation, small though it may be, to enter the fray."

"It *is* time," said Elschen, in a deep voice. She was

a celebrated German poet, so tall that seated at the table she still appeared to be standing.

"We're hoping she'll settle down one of these days," said an aunt. "She's been flitting all over the globe."

"That is good for awhile, but now she must get to work," boomed Elschen.

"We fear," said an aunt, "the problem is more than restlessness. She said she thought biographies were horrib—"

"But that won't do at all!" interrupted the publisher. Having captured everyone's attention, she paused to inspect her wineglass, holding it up to the light and turning it slowly. "Horrible?" She looked at Jieme. "I saw some of the pages you started. They showed a good deal of promise."

"We worry so much about her. She needs to stop wandering and become focused."

"True," contributed the editor. Her eyes, after glancing up briefly, went back to her plate.

Elschen said, "If you wait too long to begin, your work suffers."

Jieme had started gulping wine as soon as the conversation began to careen toward her. She was repeating to herself, "Say nothing." The more besieged she felt, the more she concentrated on the phrase. The voice inside her was shouting. Too late, she discovered she was also shouting out loud.

No one spoke so she continued more calmly, "I do have a focus, I've been working at it wherever I go."

"While you travel?" asked the publisher, still twirling her wineglass.

"What an ass," Jieme thought, hoping she wasn't speaking aloud.

"Tell us about it," everyone begged.

"I'm writing. But not biographies."

"Really. What, then?" asked Elschen.

Jieme took a deep breath. Her lungs were full of air and dread. Exhaling, she said, "Poetry."

For a few moments there was only the sound of chewing and swallowing and the clinking of silver on china.

"Poetry, did you say?" asked the publisher.

Jieme nodded. She seized her knife and began to tap the table.

"But what makes you think you can do that?" asked an aunt.

Tap tap tap.

"I didn't say I was good at it. Just, I am not wandering. I am focused." Tap tap. "So you all can stop worrying about me."

"How interesting," said Elschen, coolly. "Perhaps you have something with you?"

Jieme threw down her knife and rushed from the room.

"I'm sorry," mumbled an aunt. "This is what happened before. We are helpless."

"Well," said the publisher, "I'm sure none of us—"

Jieme reentered carrying a small notebook. She thrust it at Elschen. "Here." Then she sat and gulped another glass of wine.

The towering poet opened the notebook. She read the first page, then the second. After that, she skimmed through the rest. When she was finished she handed the notebook to an aunt sitting beside her, who repeated the process. Like a sacrament, the notebook was passed around the table in silence.

Finally, Elschen asked, "Do you want an opinion about your poems?"

Jieme was clear she did not. She shook her head and was immediately dizzy.

"Of course these are only rudimentary," Elschen commenced, "but even so, one can see problems. They are tentative, repetitious. The most serious flaw, however, is that they are quite derivative. I can find no original—"

"Yes, exactly," interjected the publisher.

"Yes," added the editor.

"—ideas or forms," continued Elschen. "You are most fortunate to be receiving a professional critique at this stage. Most people who attempt to write poetry delude themselves, thinking they are able to create important work, when in actuality they lack that essential spark of originality."

The aunts dashed upstairs and returned with armloads of books. They crowded around Jieme, their fingers flying through the pages.

"See? See here? This is just like that first poem, only—"

"Look, here. You've used the same title."

"Look at this!" An aunt was brandishing a large book. "She had genius and broke new ground. This is true poetry, don't you see?"

"Look at these rhythms, how—"

"It's the same subject but—"

In their zeal the aunts were shoving their books in Jieme's face, pushing each other and batting each other's books aside.

Jieme put two fingers in her mouth and a piercing whistle flew out, followed by words which exploded without caution: "At least I'm trying. Maybe

I'll never write one word that's any good. But look at you . . . parasites and vultures, preying on the lives of the great poets. You research everything, you . . . prove every point, you . . . mince along on tiptoe making sure you get everything right, all this quotation and footnotes . . . is that better?"

The aunts fumbled their way back to their seats.

"You're cowards!" shouted Jieme, standing up and swaying. "The mop-up act of history! I pity you. Bright, perfectionistic . . . even good writers, but where is your courage?" She suddenly realized she did feel pity for these aging writers who knew famous people, won awards, and produced shelves of books. "I'm thankful for my recklessness. Who of you would dare, who would have the hubris to think one day you might produce something original? You poor biographers, trapped in success and each other's regard. And now, to make matters worse, you're beginning to die off." Tears were running down her face.

The next day no one mentioned the dinner fiasco. Jieme packed to go. She felt the frail embraces, the dry little kisses on her cheeks, as the aunts said their good-byes. Every eye managed to look elsewhere.

A few months later Jieme was in a bookstore. An

aunt had a shining new biography prominently displayed. Jieme picked it up and opened it in the middle. Something grim and desperate reached out from the pages and clutched at her. It was so painful she couldn't even hold the book. She put it back with a shake of her head.

She felt a rush of relief at her escape, gratitude for her guardian stubbornness. She was free to write and to fail.

The Good Doctor

IN THE BACK OF THE ROOM at a medical conference a well-known neurologist, who specialized in migraine treatment, and the Good Doctor reached toward the coffeepot at the same moment.

"After you."

"No, after you."

Looking up, they read each other's nametags and their eyes opened wide in recognition. They had been hearing about each other from a mutual acquaintance, Dr. Trook, who was trying to talk them into joining her fledgling medical group.

"Dr. Fleering, we meet at last," said the neurologist.

"Ah, Dr. Zint," said the Good Doctor.

They talked during the break. They agreed that though Trook was overly interested in money, she was, at least, extremely funny. Neither thought they would join her group. But having met each other, they were a bit more inclined to do so.

Trook was pleased when she learned the two doctors had met. She invited them out to an expensive dinner.

"Tell me, Zint, how is it that you decided to become

a physician?" asked Fleering, the Good Doctor.

"I have two replies to that question, the cheerful answer and the true but sad answer. Which do you prefer?"

"The true answer."

"I had a younger sister," said Zint, "who died due to a misdiagnosis. She could have lived, had her doctors been more thorough. As a result, I felt a need to try to do something to save people. And so I became a doctor."

"Amazing," said the Good Doctor. "I, too, had a younger sister who died. She was prescribed the wrong medication by an incompetent quack. And, like you, this led me to become a doctor—exactly as you say— to try to help save others." The conversation seemed auspicious and they joined Trook's group.

Fleering sent many of her patients to Zint for consultation and treatment for their migraines. She told them Zint was the very best in her field.

The neurologist was always hearing about the Good Doctor from these patients: how they traveled long distances to see her and believed in her; how she helped them when everyone else had failed; how, if it hadn't been for her, they would have given up in despair. Even though Zint differed with a few of

Fleering's medical ideas, she saw how her patients improved. Part of their motivation to get better seemed to be their love for the Good Doctor and their desire to please her.

One day one of Fleering's patients, Ms. C——, was consulting with Zint about her headaches.

"I've never been so insulted," she said. "Last week I waited for over two hours to see Dr. Fleering. When I asked how much longer it would be, I was told in a rude way that they didn't know. I walked out and I'm never going back."

Zint said, "Why don't you tell Dr. Fleering what happened and how you are feeling."

"No, I'm through with her."

Zint saw the Good Doctor a few days later and related the conversation with Ms. C——.

Fleering responded, "I heard she made a scene in the waiting room. If she can't be polite, she should find another doctor."

This came as a shock to Zint, who was often quite indulgent with her patients; after all, they were suffering and it was understandable that they would get upset from time to time. Furthermore, Fleering's patients were always telling Zint that the Good Doctor had promised she would never abandon them for any reason. Yet it seemed she was doing just that.

The next time Ms. C— saw Zint, she repeated that she wanted a new doctor. This time Zint did not try to dissuade her.

Zint was disillusioned with the Good Doctor, and yet, it was not so simple. Zint had made peace with her need to bring back her dead sister and no longer felt compelled to be the perfect doctor. The Good Doctor had made no such peace. She was still striving for perfection, with all the resentment such an endeavor gives rise to.

Mammae Potentēs

I. In Which I Set Forth

BORED, JEALOUS OF MY FRIENDS who were constantly travelling and bragging of their adventures, and having always been drawn to the romance of the sea, I mustered what courage I had and went down to the quays in search of a ship's passage. I wandered up and down, approaching one vessel after another. Possessing no seafaring skills, I was invariably turned away.

I spied a small sailing boat moored some distance from the others. A few crew members appeared to be readying the craft for departure, while a woman sat on deck strumming a guitar.

"Halloo," I called out.

The guitarist glanced at me and stopped playing.

"Could you direct me to the captain?"

"Speaking."

"Ah, Captain, are you, by chance, seeking any additional crew?"

"No, full up."

"Do you, perchance, know of a ship that could use a willing hand?"

"I don't mingle with the other ships." She began to stroke the strings again.

I heard an anguished shout. I looked up to see someone falling through the air. A moment later she hit the deck with a thud. Everyone rushed over. She was breathing.

"Take her to a hospital," the captain ordered a crew member. Then she looked at me. "Looks like we might need someone after all. What's your sailing experience?"

"I've read a lot of books and I will do anything at all for no pay."

"You can start by finishing up there."

I had no notion of the task but I scrambled up the mast as fast as I could go. A few hours later, upon the return of the hand who had taken the woman to a hospital, we set out.

I could see I was being given the most distasteful chores, but I performed them with goodwill and was soon accepted into the group. After awhile, feeling more at ease, I attempted to strike up a conversation with the Captain, who was still on deck playing the guitar. "Pray, where are we headed?"

"In a southerly direction."

"What is our destination?"

"Toward the south. And the purpose of the trip I don't plan to discuss." Nor would any of the crew. It was impossible to be upset, however, as the weather held fair and we prospered in a following wind. I felt more capable with every passing hour, ready for any adventure.

On the third morning the wind increased; we were flying over the waves. Suddenly we were assaulted with drenching rain, gale winds, and lashing waves. We struggled to lower the sails, which were flapping like manic wings. Then the mast snapped and, sails fluttering, flew off in the wind. The boat was more than horizontal; the keel bobbed skyward over and over. We held on with all our might. The vessel righted itself but it was taking on water at a great rate; soon we were forced to abandon ship. We jumped into the lifeboat. Moments later the ship disappeared from view.

Though we put all our strength into it, we could not bring the lifeboat toward shore and were thrust out farther and farther into the crashing black sea. Our compass was our only guide as the lifeboat tossed and twisted. A moment of decision came: whether to continue in a futile effort toward land, drift ever outward hoping blindly for rescue, or try our luck at swimming. With scarcely a thought I jumped into the maelstrom. As for the others, I knew not what choices they made. I was immediately lost among the swells. Not much later I was knocked unconscious.

II. In Which I Find Myself in an Unknown Land

WHEN I CAME TO, I was lying on my back on a cool wet surface. I opened my eyes and was blinded by sun in a blue sky. My view was intermittently darkened and my mouth held open and breath forced into me, while pressure bore down repeatedly on my chest. I struggled and sat up, coughing violently, whereupon a shout went up, followed by applause.

My eyesight was blurred but I could see I was on a beach which extended to the horizon in either direction. I could detect some shapes on it moving at a leisurely pace; other shapes were motionless on the sand; and still other smaller shapes were moving quickly about. To one side of me, the ocean was calm and beautiful, to the other, large buildings stood in a row. A crowd was gathering around me.

"Are you okay?" asked the person who had been breathing into my mouth.

I was delighted to discover she spoke my language. "Indeed," I coughed.

"Come with me," said my rescuer. She took my arm and helped me to stand. I staggered beside her as she pulled me toward the building closest to us. We entered and stepped down into a sunken room. One wall was a window facing back toward the ocean. The water seemed so close it might burst into the room at any minute. She guided me up a few steps into another room where, on a large table, were laid out many delicacies. I was plied with food. My vision was still bleary but I made out a green paste on flat yellow triangles; and vegetables and seafood inside cylinders of rice, wrapped in something like salty black paper. I was also given a drink from a loudly hissing machine. I devoured the delicious food and drink and began to revive.

"You poor thing, you must be starved," said my benefactor.

"Assuredly," I replied, around a huge mouthful of green paste.

"When you finish eating, why don't you take a hot shower. The bathroom's down the hall."

After stuffing myself with paste and rice cylinders, I found my way to a large bathroom. I stepped down into a tiled area where warm streams of water enveloped me. Healing unguents had been left out. Some I rubbed onto my burned and ravaged flesh, others I applied to my ruined hair. Clothing had also been set out: a small tight garment and a large loose one of tufted white material. This was fortunate since my own clothing was reduced to a few torn rags. I found my way back to the door to the beach.

Outside, I saw bright colors.

"Over here!" I heard my protector's familiar voice. Approaching, I saw that she was in a grove of huge umbrella-like objects. I sank down in the shade and fell asleep.

I was awakened by a sharp blow on my head. My eyes sprang open. While sleeping, my eyesight had improved: everything was now in focus.

I beheld my hostess poised above me. I surmised that she had leaned over to adjust the umbrella and accidentally struck me with her enormous breasts. She didn't seem aware of the wallop she had given me and I deemed it best to say nothing.

I sat up. I was in the midst of what appeared to be a social gathering. Something about the situation unnerved me; it took a moment before I realized the cause of my unease: everyone was extremely thin, yet had gigantic breasts. There was no sagging; all breasts pointed straight ahead. Not knowing the customs of the land, I did not allow my gaze to linger on this curious state of affairs.

They asked me questions about my origin. I was alarmed to discover I could remember almost nothing. Here and there I came upon a flash of memory, but much was a turmoil of half-formed thoughts. I was not even sure of my name.

The women were whispering and nodding and breaking into smiles.

"We've decided on a name for you," said my patroness. "Flat One."

In truth I did not like it. However, I was a guest and made no protest.

My hostess, Ruvonne, offered shelter in her house until I was rested and able to decide what next to do. I was deeply grateful, for she also provided me with food and every other necessity that might be required by someone utterly cast up and without means or provisions.

The next day she invited me to go with her to her place of work. We moved slowly in a vehicle along a wide thoroughfare, packed fore and aft, port and starboard, with other vehicles moving in the same direction. She used the time to apply various colors to her face. Arriving at her workplace, we were let in through a gate.

III. In Which I Encounter Work and Lunch

WE WENT INTO HER OFFICE. Ruvonne busied herself at her desk while I wandered around the room inspecting likenesses of faces on the walls. A buzzer sounded and my hostess motioned for me to follow her. On the way into the office next to hers, she whispered, "I work for a big producer."

There was no time to ask the meaning of the phrase. A moment later the big producer herself, Lyze, extended her hand to me in greeting and introduced herself.

I gaped in surprise. She was the thinnest woman with the largest breasts I had yet encountered. After asking several questions about my origin, and listening to my feeble attempts at recollection, she announced in a commanding tone, "Come with me to lunch, Flat One."

A subtle change appeared to be taking place: Ruvonne was relinquishing me to her superior. As best I could ascertain, I was now the big producer's property, perhaps a pet. Lyze and I climbed into the back of a long black vehicle. Once again we joined the armada moving in stately unison.

We were delivered to a tall transparent building. The midday sun glinted blindingly off its walls. Inside, the air was cool and fragrant. The room was a huge atrium filled with exotic plants. A waterfall splashed from ceiling to floor. At various levels, tables were sequestered in the foliage. Waiters bearing trays moved to and fro on a curving staircase.

We were taken to a table shaded by flowering vines, where another large-breasted woman was already seated. On seeing us she stood up; she and Lyze lightly embraced while kissing into the air.

"I'd like you to meet my newest acquaintance," said Lyze, "a shipwreck survivor who goes by the name of Flat One." It seemed the name was to follow me everywhere. "She's still in shock from her ordeal."

"Flat One, meet Fleck."

When the two women shed the dark coverings over their eyes, I received a jolt. I recalled that in my homeland, when people gathered in a beautiful place anticipating wonderful food, their eyes often sparkled. But the four eyes at my table held the same expression: unfocussed yet determined, superficially friendly but calculating. Something about the situation was vaguely familiar.

A waiter appeared. I was grateful when Lyze took it upon herself to order for me; nothing on the menu was recognizable. The waiter returned promptly and poured drinks for us from various bottles. The liquids turned out to be highly prized varieties of water.

The meal arrived, colorful little stacks of vegetation. The food was delicious but even then no glint of appreciation lit any eye. Between sips of water and tiny bites of leaves and roots, a discussion ensued.

"About the property—" began Lyze.

"Yes," said Fleck, "we think one-point-two—"

"Cut the crap, my dear," interrupted Lyze in a caressing tone. "That thing has been gathering dust for three-and-a-half years."

"But darling," countered Fleck, "we can hang onto it for another three-and-a-half years if we want to."

"Four-fifty and that's generous. Don't you have some salaries to meet?"

"Since I hold you in such esteem, I'm prepared to consider one-point-one-five. I'll even throw in the costume designs."

"Keep your doodles. I happen to know that no one else is eyeing your little bee-hind at the moment."

"You might be surprised."

It came to me, suddenly, where I had seen such eyes before: on notices in the post office for wanted criminals. Wary, lusterless, humorless eyes. I was eating lunch with criminals!

Sated with vegetables and growing sleepy, I watched an iridescent bug walk across my plate. The conversation buzzed along, harsh words swaddled in gentle tones.

" . . . Five hundred and a handshake," Lyze was saying.

Fleck lifted her goblet of water. "Skoal."

"Gesundheit."

Back at the studio I took a nap on one of the hide-covered couches in Lyze's office. In the late afternoon she invited—or perhaps ordered—me to accompany her to the spa.

IV. In Which I Visit a Place of Relaxation

I FOLLOWED HER ACROSS A PAVED AREA into a low building. In a mirrored room we stripped off our clothes and wrapped towels around our torsos. We entered a steaming room where several women were half-submerged in a fiercely bubbling pool. A few others sat at the pool's edge, dangling their feet in the roiling water. Many had shed their towels. I was face to face with the local breasts.

It was both disturbing and awe-inspiring. The breasts stood at attention, almost saluted, glistening and effulgent. I could see the women stealing glances at my diminutive offerings, obvious even under the towel, with something like pity in their eyes. The spa culture was to be silent. It was just as well; I was weary of Flat One introductions.

As we soaked, understanding dawned: the mammoth appendages were not for beauty, nor even for attracting attention. Their purpose was akin to that of the outlaws of old, who swaggered around town with two loaded pistols, ready to draw and fire at the slightest provocation. In this land of criminals, one needed something for self-protection and for putting teeth, as it were, into one's own threats.

I glanced at Lyze, trying to imagine her without her arsenal. She would have looked almost waiflike with her thin neck and limbs. But toting her magnums she gave notice of readiness for combat.

The pulsing hot water was pleasurable, but I was relieved when Lyze nodded toward me and we stood up to go.

151

We were standing under sprays of water. "You stick out around here like a sore thumb," said Lyze.

"Oh, are you referring to these?" I was trying to maintain levity but my voice cracked.

"You've had a tough break, with the shipwreck and all. I've decided to do something nice for you. After lunch I had my surgeon called, the one who produced my stunners." She glanced down. "She agreed, as a favor to me, to see you this afternoon."

"See me . . . about what sort of matter?" I croaked.

"Just a quick discussion. She's probably too busy to start on you today." Lyze appeared as determined to prevail in this endeavor as in the battle of lunch.

v. A Terrifying Episode

MY STOMACH CLENCHED WITH FEAR. In desperation I did the first thing that came to mind: I clutched in the vicinity of my heart and moaned pitiably. It was not a complete ruse; my heart was galloping.

"Hold on," said Lyze, rushing from the room.

I seized my chance to escape. I grabbed a pile of towels and dashed outside. I saw a pair of huge urns on pedestals. Hoping for the best, I pitched the towels into the nearer of the two and scrambled in after them. Inside, it was empty except for some dirt and a few dead leaves.

I heard a mob arrive.

"She'll never get away," said a grim voice I recognized as the big producer's.

"I hope she's okay. She was pretty weak yesterday." This was Ruvonne.

The voices were coming nearer. The mob was right under the urn. I held my breath.

"She won't be okay when I get through with her. Where the hell did she go?"

"You're sure she was feeling alright at the spa?"

"She's an ingrate."

I shivered in my urn. Unwelcome images popped into my mind, of what a mob of criminals might do to an ingrate. Finally the voices moved on.

I wrapped up in the towels and huddled until nightfall. Huge lights sliced back and forth across the sky like terrible swift swords. Part of the search, I surmised.

I popped my head up. I had a view of the entrance gate. Two uniformed women were on guard, sipping from small cans. The gates opened to let in a vehicle. It was time to flee.

One towel draped around my neck, I climbed out of the urn. I was spotted immediately.

"Look, isn't that her?"

"No doubt about it." Raucous laughter followed this comment.

The guards started toward me. My recent ordeal notwithstanding, fear endowed me with agility and speed. I dodged and feinted between the guards, squeezed through the closing gate, and dashed to freedom.

I crossed a wide road and fled into a grove of trees. The guards were close behind, sweeping their flashlights to and fro.

I rushed wildly among the trees, finally stopping behind a wide trunk when the ache in my side was unbearable and my lungs were bursting.

The guards came toward my tree.

"See her come this way?"

"Think so."

"What's the big deal, anyway?"

"You know the boss. Probably wants to sign her." Sign? I could only guess at the meaning of that chilling word. I shuddered at their mirth.

They stood in silence for a minute.

"Hell with it."

"Yeah, let's go."

I collapsed momentarily with relief. But I wanted more distance from those cold eyes and heavy armaments. I started walking alongside the road. I used the towel to wave at a passing vehicle. It veered over and stopped. Several large-breasted young women were inside.

vi. In Which I Use Cunning and Ingenuity

"HEY, YOU OKAY?"

"To a certain degree."

"What's up?"

"I am in need of a ride to the beach."

This seemed to put them at ease. "Some party, huh?"

I thought it best to be affirmative. "Indeed."

"Hop in."

When we arrived at the beach, I confessed. "It pains me to admit that there is no party."

"Hey, we'll find one. Stick around."

"I must attend to something."

"You need some clothes?"

"Most assuredly, I do."

Once again I was the recipient of the generosity of the denizens of this unusual land. They each made a contribution. Though the effect was somewhat haphazard, it was a great comfort to be dressed again.

"Sure you don't want to stick with us?"

"Unfortunately I must deal with an urgent matter that cannot be postponed."

"Hey, good luck."

I walked down from the road to the beach. I made my way along the sand until I came to a pier. By then it was early morning. Some fishing boats were preparing to set out.

"In which direction are you headed?" I asked at the first boat.

"Up the coast, mate. North."

I was still unable to remember the name of my homeland, but I knew the boat was traveling on the desired compass course. "Could you use a hand?"

"Sorry, mate."

"I'll work for my passage, do anything asked of me. I've been employed on ships before."

"Ever been on a fishing boat?"

"Countless times."

"Okay, sailor. No pay and no complaints. And you bunk on deck."

The voyage commenced. Before she turned around, the captain connected me with another vessel. In this manner I made my way northward.

After further adventures and delays, during which memory returned, I at last arrived in my homeland.

Friends greeted me with tears of joy. They had thought I perished in the storm. They wanted to hold a big celebration to honor my return, but I demurred. I still feared Lyze. Who could be certain of the limits of her power?

Fog

JIT THE FARMER LIVED IN A PLACE that was always dark and gloomy. She could never see more than a few feet in any direction. One day when she was out walking, she noticed that one leg was more fully extended than the other.

"What can this mean?" she wondered. "Either my legs are two different lengths or the ground is uneven."

She decided to turn toward the more bent leg and continue walking, to find out what would happen. After awhile she observed the air growing brighter. Colors were more vivid: the sky was a bluish color.

She turned around and looked behind her; below was a valley filled with dense fog. But above the fog the air was clear and the sunlight was brilliant.

"I will build a hut and start a life in the sun."

Later she missed her home and started back down into the valley. After a few steps the colors faded, the blue sky disappeared, dreariness returned.

But something was different. "This gloom is a narrow layer with sun above it, rather than the condition that pervades the world."

She was happier in this new darkness.

A Guardian of the Perimeter

THE METROPOLIS PULSED AT THE VERY CENTER of the nation, the nexus of all modernity and sophistication, the climax of all riches and technology. Within its splendor were countless subcultures. Ours was a band of high-spirited artists and intellectuals, blessed with lives of ease.

At the center of our circle was Jae, the liveliest and most inventive of us all. Her fervor inspired us; whenever she set out on a new project, we fell over ourselves to follow. Such were her gifts, her fame began to spread throughout the metropolis, as the dazzling brilliance of her potential gave way to the steady glow of her achievements.

We were stunned when she disappeared. We looked for her everywhere. Then we convinced ourselves she was off on a secret adventure and would regale us with stories of her escapades when she returned.

After awhile we grew tired of waiting. Without Jae to inspire and guide us, our days lost their glamour. Enthusiasm dissipated into irritability and boredom. We had always assumed our futures, though undetermined, would be bright. But as time went by, we sensed a dimming of our prospects. Something in us was unfulfilled, some longing, some question haunted us which we could neither formulate nor answer.

One day when we were languishing at our usual café, an official-looking messenger came over to our table. She handed us a large envelope, saying, "The government requests your assistance. Please deliver this important document to your colleague, Jae. Our attempts have been unsuccessful but we are hopeful you will prevail—"

"But we don't know where she is."

"We have located her. She is at the perimeter."

Nothing could have surprised us more.

The metropolis is surrounded by a band of factories. This band, in turn, is encircled by a broad region of farmlands. Around everything is the vast ring of the buffer zone, a bleak unrelieved wasteland. At the outermost edge of the buffer zone lies, some say, the perimeter, a boundary against losses and encroachments.

There has always been controversy regarding the existence of the perimeter. Among believers, there are those who feel it should be guarded. None of us had ever given any thought to the matter. Nor, to our knowledge, had Jae.

The messenger presented us with a second envelope. "This contains a map, rail tickets, a list of necessary supplies, and funds. Do you have any questions?"

We were too stunned to reply. We shook our heads. The messenger nodded and departed. We tore open the envelope and seized the map. The place marked "J" was indeed at the perimeter, at one of its most inhospitable reaches.

"She's at the very edge!" someone wailed. "I've never even been outside the metropolis!"

Nor had any of us.

"Do you think she's in danger?"

"Maybe we should find out what's in her letter." But we were daunted by its huge seal. Whatever was about to happen, there was no denying that our lives were again infused with excitement, and Jae, once more, was the cause.

Two days later we gathered at the train station on a remote platform for trains outbound. Then the metropolis was behind us and we were rushing past smokestacks and huge factories. These gave way to fields and orchards. We changed to another train and continued our outward journey.

Expecting the barren buffer zone, we were surprised to enter an area of bustling activity: workers pouring foundations, hoisting the skeletal beginnings of new buildings, raising power lines, lowering huge sections of pipe.

When we passed beyond this industry, the land grew desolate: hills covered in gorse, water collecting in the valley basins. The sky changed to a doleful gray. We dozed off.

We were awakened by a shriek of brakes. It was the end of the line. When we climbed down, the train reversed itself and departed.

Nothing moved or made a sound.

We set out across the dreary terrain with map and compass. Our spirits sagged with uncertainty and dread. Could Jae have survived the harsh indifference of this land? The sky darkened, we shivered in a chill breeze, our spirits sank further. When it was too murky to go on, we made camp. We gobbled a tasteless meal in the gloom and fell into uneasy sleep.

The next morning, enveloped in dense fog, we had to rely solely on our compass. We marched in silence. Over the course of the day, the fog lifted and was replaced by the relentless grayness of the day before.

Then, when hope was gone and light was fading, we spied a small dark speck ahead. As we came nearer, the speck grew into a rough cabin with smoke rising from a chimney. We ran toward it, shouting.

The door opened and a figure emerged. It was Jae—but there was no welcome, no smile, no sparkle in her eyes. "I wondered if you might come here someday," was all she said.

We grew quiet, our relief tempered by confusion.

Inside the cabin a stove and candles gave the only light. We brought out our stores of food and wine, resolved to create what gaiety we could. We gave Jae her envelope; she read it and said nothing.

"What does it say?" we implored.

"I'll tell you tomorrow."

Eventually our determination and wine brought a semblance of former days. Jae was with us and the circle was complete. But instead of the irreverence and laughter of earlier times, we made confessions, talked of disappointments and failures.

Jae listened; occasionally she said a word or two. There was a stillness about her, as if the silence of the heath had entered her, transforming her into a being half-human, half-landscape.

As we talked into the night, candles flickering, some burden was lifted from us, something was freed to expand in our chests, allowing us to breathe more deeply. We slept on the floor, our sleeping bags pressed together, our hearts at peace at last.

We were awakened by scents of breakfast. Jae rushed us along, then told us to pack. She made a large pack for herself.

Outside, the morning was damp and chilly. Jae tramped quickly ahead of us. She jumped the narrow streams and set stones to cross the wide ones. Breathless with exertion, blistered and sore, we struggled to keep up. She halted after several hours and set down her pack.

"Turn around and look back," said Jae.

We discovered we had gradually been climbing and were now on a rounded elevation. We saw the dark speck of her cabin. Raising our eyes to the horizon, we saw something else, other dark shapes, barely visible.

"Let's rest."

We sat down. As before, the oppressive land quelled speech and merriment. Jae remained standing. She pulled the envelope from her pack and held it awhile, tantalizing us almost beyond endurance. Was this a glimmer of her old sly humor?

At last she spoke. "From the train you saw buildings going up. They are what you now see on the horizon, the suburbs of a new metropolis. The center will be near here." Indicating the letter with a nod, she added, "I have been asked to be mayor."

Our hearts lifted in joy and amazement. Jae again leading us, leader of the new metropolis! In a moment our histories rearranged: everything had been leading up to this; our time of aimlessness was over. How could we ever have doubted that our lives would be glorious? Of course Jae would save us!

We cheered.

Jae lifted up her pack and slung it on her back. "Report that I decline. There must be a new perimeter. I shall remain a guardian."

She turned and descended. She proceeded swiftly, further into the wild land, across the next valley and up and over a crest of hill. She reemerged on a distant hill. She reached the top and went on and we saw her no more.

Paying Attention

Wyr lived with her aunts, who thought she was odd. They were cold to her and indicated that they tolerated her only out of obligation. Most of the time she didn't mind.

Her cousin Cril came for a visit. Cril was cheerful and always laughing. Wyr liked her. She wanted her cousin to like her, too. For several days Wyr thought about how to impress her cousin. At last she arrived at a plan: she would listen hard to everything Cril said and learn about her. Wyr felt good; her lungs filled and her chest felt lighter

Whenever Cril spoke, Wyr sat still in order to let her cousin's words come in. But despite her efforts, she was not able to follow what her cousin was saying. This was typical: words usually jumbled together and she would drift off. Even though it happened over and over, Wyr continued her efforts. She really did want to be quiet and learn.

One day Wyr understood something Cril said. The words pierced into her mind with great clarity, like a beacon into darkness: Cril was afraid of snakes. At last Wyr knew something useful. She reminded herself of her new information over and over. She felt close to Cril; they were probably friends now. What should she do with her wonderful knowledge?

Cril turned down the covers of her bed and started screaming. A snake lay on the sheet. The aunts, hearing the screams, rushed into the room.

"What is it?" they asked, with desperate concern. They saw the snake and screamed, too.

A few moments later they looked at the snake again. They slowly moved their heads closer until they could see it was a toy made of wood. "How could this have happened?" The aunts were bewildered. They decided, "It must be Wyr."

Something was pushing Wyr back and forth. She woke up. The aunts were at her bedside, shouting. Now they were pulling her up out of bed and dragging her down the hall.

Where were they going? To Cril's room. Suddenly Wyr remembered; a bolt of pleasure coursed through her. Why were the aunts so upset? They were in her cousin's room now and Cril looked upset, too.

"Why did you put this here?" demanded Cril.

Wyr started to smile. It was time to explain. Where were the words? She hunted in her mind, but it was

167

like looking through empty rooms. Something good was supposed to happen. What was it?

Something was going wrong. Why was Cril crying? Why were the aunts on their knees, talking to her cousin and looking miserable? Cril was crying harder. Now Cril was moving quickly around the room throwing things into her suitcase. She was running out of the room.

The front door opened and slammed shut.

The aunts were even more aloof. They barely spoke to Wyr and sent her meals to her room. Wyr remembered going to the store. She had seen the snake. It was exactly what she was looking for. She remembered putting it in Cril's bed, almost laughing. Why hadn't her cousin known the reason for the trick? It was to show that she had paid attention.

Didn't anyone understand? That was what tricks were for.

The Triumphant One

IN THE OTHERWISE UNATTRACTIVE TOWN of **B**— there was one beautiful house. Its proportions were graceful, flowering vines spilled from balcony to balcony. It belonged to the *emerita* professor and historian, Doña Ternilla.

The house contained a small but exquisite collection of ancient objects which the Professor had gathered over the years. A vicious watchdog patrolled the premises.

Ternilla had a reputation for equal ferocity: at the university she had terrorized both students and colleagues with her biting words. When she left, she withdrew to her house to be alone with her collection.

Some have said the center of **B**— was its rather plain cathedral, but most, if asked, would have said it was the Jácara, a tavern with a wide, graceless patio. Many of the townspeople gathered there almost daily.

One group—the town doctor, judge, civil engineer, and *fiscal*—was at its usual table on the patio, sharing a bottle of wine.

"Did you hear about Ternilla's burglary?" asked

Doctor Burga, lifting her glass and smiling with delight. "Shocking."

"Incredible," replied Judge Frente. "Who would have been reckless enough to try to rob her, of all people. And how did they ever get away with it?"

"A cat burglar would have been attacked by the dog," said Doña Merma, the civil engineer.

"The dog—and worse!" laughed the *fiscal*, Echada.

The next day there was more excitement at the Jácara. "I'm absolutely stunned," said Doctor Burga. "La Caradura! I thought I would go to my grave—"

"And red-handed!" interrupted Judge Frente, rubbing her hands together in delight. "Oh, this will be a delicious trial!"

"How could she have been so careless? Caught with Ternilla's artifacts, it's unbelievable—" began Merma.

Echada jumped in. "Overconfidence. I see it all the time. Too much success for too long."

"As far as I'm concerned, La Caradura is a national treasure. Her escapades have thrilled me all my life," said Burga.

"It's fitting, though, isn't it," said Echada, "that the Professor's artifacts should be the ones to bring her down. La Caradura only steals the best from the best. And Ternilla's collection is—was—certainly that."

170

"I was absolutely certain she could never be caught. It's been one of the axioms of my philosophy. Really, I'm quite upset," sighed Burga.

With that, the party sank into quietude.

The first day of the trial, business in B— came to a standstill. Everyone who could, squeezed into the courtroom. The bar and patio of the Jácara took in the overflow.

Judge Frente was on the panel and Echada was prosecuting, so they were assured positions of prominence. Merma stayed firmly in her seat in the gallery, but Burga lost hers the minute she got up to attend to an emergency. The mood was festive. After several calls to order, the trial began.

Later, Echada was concluding her opening statement: " . . . You will see a stunning array of treasures standing in mute but dazzling witness to the virtually limitless crimes of the accused. You will see with great clarity this brilliant, soulless criminal. I am certain you will find her guilty, and deserving of the most severe punishment allowed."

Not everyone could fit into the Jácara that evening, so drinks were brought to the throng outside. The judge and prosecutor had absented themselves for the time being; Burga and Merma were sitting on the curb.

"You think La Caradura should go to prison for life?" asked the doctor. "I don't agree. A lesser sentence would be more fitting. Just think of the entertainment she has provided over the years."

"But what of the people she robbed?"

"That horrible Professor Ternilla? And the other snobs?" Burga paused a moment. "They probably got what they deserved."

When the trial was over a few days later, the group reconvened at their table.

"I thought the Professor was going to have a stroke on the spot!" said Burga. "Have you ever seen anyone so angry? I was perched on the edge of my seat, ready to rush forward."

"What a witness!" laughed Echada. "I half-feared she'd suddenly turn on me and start listing my own crimes. I'd go to prison for sure."

"I've never seen such rage," nodded the judge, "in or out of the courtroom. Maybe that's why she stays so aloof. I expect we'll never hear from her again."

"So it's life imprisonment for our thief. I'm sorry it's over," sighed Burga.

"Still, it's fair," said Merma.

Ever since the burglary, Doña Ternilla had been

wandering around her house. The robbery had been the most devastating event of her life. She looked at the velvet pillow on which an ancient belt clasp had lain; now there was only its impression in the deep nap of the fabric. She gazed at the wall where a priceless sword had hung on silver hooks; now the polished hooks held nothing. A few of her artifacts had been found at the time of the arrest; several had not.

After the trial she mumbled to herself, "My testimony was brilliant. And yet, was everyone snickering just a little? Oh, who cares what the fools think." Then a new thought occurred to her: "Maybe there's a way I can retrieve all my treasures."

She sent her lawyer to the prison to speak to La Caradura. The thief refused to see her. The lawyer tried a few more times with the same result.

"The insolent wretch," Ternilla muttered. "I'll go myself."

A guard stood outside La Caradura's cell. "You have another visitor." The thief was reading. She waited awhile, then, with drawling condescension, asked who it was. "Doña Ternilla," answered the guard.

"Ah, the angry one. Perhaps I shall give her a moment, even so." She read for a little while longer.

The Professor was sitting in the visitors' room behind a thick grate. The thief sat down on the other side.

Ternilla tried to say something, but, on seeing the hated face, she became so furious she could not speak.

La Caradura, uncharacteristically, uttered the first words, "Good day, Professor," in a low, mocking tone.

Ternilla, finding her voice, shouted back, "Devil, where are my things? Tell me, beast!"

La Caradura stood. She spat and walked away. The Professor left, fuming.

The next day the Professor was pacing and talking to herself. "Was I too impulsive at the prison? The monster did say 'Good day.' Should I go back? It's my only chance to retrieve my treasures. What use could she have for them?"

Professor and thief were on either side of the grate. Both were silent. It appeared to be a contest to see who could show the greatest *altiveza*.

Ternilla was the first to surrender. She cleared her throat. "Good day," she rasped.

"Good day," came the measured reply.

There was a long pause. "Pray, where are my missing objects?"

"I don't care to discuss it," said the prisoner.

"What do you mean?" There was another pause.

"Worthless filth, I'm wasting my time with you."

And so the second visit ended.

Doña Ternilla received a fat envelope—from the prison! It contained a strange letter from La Caradura: the thief went on at length about one of the Professor's artifacts, the jeweled sixth century belt clasp.

Ternilla was outraged. What was this? Gloating? Later she read the letter again. The Professor was grudgingly impressed with the thief's knowledge and appreciation of the piece.

Another letter arrived. This one contained a recitation of the history of the ancient sword and praises for its craftsmanship. "What can she be up to?" wondered the Professor. "No good." She threw the letters away.

From time to time she received other letters from the prison. It was infuriating, these treatises on her possessions. Nonetheless, she felt compelled to read each one. She was beginning to feel something like admiration for the thief's expertise, in spite of herself.

The Professor was debating the purchase of a gold Roman fibula. She knew the rarity and excellence of the piece and wanted it, but she also knew that the seller was asking too high a price. They went back and forth. Suddenly matters were complicated by the appearance of a second buyer.

"What should I do?" worried the Professor. "This is ridiculous. I've been making these decisions all my life. Either I pay the price or I turn it down." Yet she found herself wanting to consult with an experienced collector, someone who could help her weigh the forces of desire and prudence.

Feeling ridiculous, she headed toward the prison. "What would a thief know of haggling for a good price?" she muttered to herself.

La Caradura came to the visitors' room immediately. Her demeanor had changed: she was almost cordial. "Good day, Professor."

"I am here on a rather unusual mission," said Ternilla, with some embarrassment. She then related her predicament regarding the fibula.

La Caradura listened carefully. "How badly do you want it?"

"Very much."

"How will you feel if the other buyer gets it, assuming there actually is another buyer."

"Terribly upset."

"And what is the price of your peace of mind, that is, over and above the price of the object?"

"Well, it is something."

"I think that is how you should consider the matter."

The Professor felt a moment of confused gratitude. She started to thank the thief; instead she stood up and rushed out.

There were further letters from La Caradura and further visits to the prison. A discussion began of ancient history and its treasures. The visits became a daily occurrence.

The Professor had given up on the idea of locating her possessions, but she began to feel she had found something compensatory: never in her life had she encountered anyone with such a kindred interest and depth of knowledge. Soon she was telling the thief of other treasures hidden in a new vault. She spoke of her regrets, of objects not purchased when the opportunity was at hand; she confessed her dreams, of artifacts she might acquire someday.

La Caradura, too, spoke of things coveted, obtained, lost.

The Professor was at home, mulling over her latest conversation with the thief. "I have known people less despicable, but never have I known anyone as intelligent. Could it be that I have finally met my equal?"

A peculiar desire began to haunt the Professor, a question she wanted to ask. It made no sense. She attempted to push it away but it would not leave.

At a subsequent visit with the prisoner, she found herself saying, half-holding her breath, "There is something I must ask you. I must know, did you find my house the most beautiful, and my collection the most impressive, of all?"

La Caradura reflected and then replied, "To be sure, both your house and your collection are the finest I have ever seen, reflecting the most exquisite taste imaginable."

"Ah," the Professor exhaled, confused by the intensity of her relief. But doubts returned. The Professor was driven to ask her question again and again.

La Caradura tirelessly reassured her.

Then a new thought began to plague the Professor: perhaps the brilliant criminal was merely using her, trying to find out the location of her storage vault.

"Would you like to know where I keep my objects now?" she asked at the next visit.

The thief's voice was full of regret. "What would be the point, since I am condemned to spend my life in prison."

The Professor felt ashamed. But a few moments later she felt compelled to ask, "Are you sure you don't care about my storage vault? Perhaps I will tell you where it is." She wondered to herself, "Why am I saying this? Am I bewitched?"

"Please do not bother," came the weary reply.

Eventually the Professor found herself telling the thief about the vault. The disclosure did not provide the satisfaction she had expected. "What is it I want?" she asked herself. "What is this strange need I have, to go to her and tell her everything?"

"It is alright," said the thief, when the Professor had revealed even these troubling thoughts. "I understand our bond."

"Yes, exactly," said the Professor, comforted at last.

In the convent on the outskirts of town, the mother superior was pacing in anger. "Call in the next one," she ordered the departing sister, who was shriveled from her interrogation.

"Yes, Mother."

The next poor sister entered the room.

"Tell me, what do you know of the matter?"

"Nothing, Mother."

"When did you last look in the cabinet?"

"Why, it's been years, I believe."

"Was the goblet there at the time?"

"Yes, I remember it distinctly."

"This is very important. Did you remember to lock the cabinet afterwards?"

Why, Mother, I was with you at the time. You had the key and locked it yourself."

"And you have not been in the cabinet since?"

"No, Mother."

"Call the next one."

"Yes, Mother."

The mother superior was becoming convinced that only a skilled thief could have taken the precious goblet. She spoke to the convent lawyer about her suspicion—that La Caradura was the one responsible for the theft. The lawyer besieged the prisoner by letter and visit but the thief did not deign to respond.

At the Jácara, Judge Frente was holding forth. "It never stops, this La Caradura business. Now it's the goblet affair at the convent. Today I capitulated: I ordered the thief to divulge the location of the goblet, or prison would become more unpleasant."

"But how do you know she took it?" asked Merma.

"I don't. But the mother superior will not leave me alone. This will give me some respite, at least."

The following evening the tavern was abuzz with new gossip.

"I can't believe it, La Caradura confessed!" said Burga, her eyes round with excitement.

"Is it true she drew a map?" asked Merma.

"With an X to mark where she hid the goblet," said Frente. "So you see, my order has proven fruitful."

"What could have possessed her to capitulate so quickly?" wondered Burga.

"Prison has worn her down," said Echada. "It does, you know. Everyone loses their nerve."

"Even La Caradura? The thought saddens me," sighed the doctor.

When the convent lawyer and her assistants attempted to follow the map, they became hopelessly lost. The lawyer went back to the prison and the thief contemptuously redrew the map. Again the group lost their way. Three more times this happened, with each side growing more exasperated.

The mother superior made another petition: since La Caradura was so inept at mapmaking, could she be put under heavy guard and allowed to lead the lawyer to the goblet?

It seemed the whole town was at the prison gates, waiting to catch sight of the famous thief. A few determined citizens had camped out the night before, some had arrived before dawn, the rest had come early in the morning to jostle their way to a good spot for viewing.

"That's her!"

"That's a guard, you fool."

"Look! How bent over she has gotten."

"That's a prison laundress."

It was early afternoon when the lawyer and a bevy of assistants emerged from the prison doors and headed across an open space toward the gate.

Next, a group of heavily armed guards appeared. The crowd began pushing against the gates, craning their necks.

"There she is!"

This time it was La Caradura, handcuffed in the middle of the guards, her bearing as proud as ever.

A cheer went up.

"Out of the way!" ordered a guard as she unlocked the gate. The guards pushed the mob aside and hastened the prisoner away.

When some of the townspeople started to follow, a guard turned and shouted, "Disperse, now!"

La Caradura directed the entourage into the old town, a warren of arcades, narrow alleys, and tunnels. Impatiently, she urged everyone to move faster and faster. They went this way and that. Hadn't they been here just a moment ago? Perhaps it was another street. Suddenly she was gone.

There was a jubilant mood in the tavern that evening; it was crowded with townspeople laughing and shouting. The group was at their table.

"What an escapade!" laughed Burga.

"My position forbids me to comment," said Judge Frente, a faint smile at the corners of her mouth.

"What were you thinking, letting her out?" demanded Echada.

"You can't imagine the pressure I was under. The mother superior simply would not stop hounding me. Frankly, it's something of a relief."

"I'm delighted," grinned Burga, lifting her glass. "Our hero roams free again!"

Weeks passed, the search for the prisoner dwindled away, and interest shifted to other matters. There were no reports of burglaries that resembled La Caradura's methods.

She had vanished.

The Professor had resented the intrusion of the convent lawyer and been gratified by La Caradura's scorn.

She had delighted in the lawyer's failure to understand the maps.

When she learned of the plan to release the prisoner under guard, she was struck by such an inchoate mixture of feelings, she could barely sleep or eat. She did not come to the gate. That whole day she stayed in bed with a blinding headache.

On hearing of the thief's escape, the Professor's heart lifted in excitement. Then it fell. Her *confidenta* was gone. For the first time in her life she felt painfully alone. She shut herself in her house with her books and correspondence while the hunt went on. She grew pale and ill.

After the search for the prisoner subsided, Ternilla could not find her balance: she felt weighed down by sorrow and, at the same time, lifted up by a dizzying emptiness.

A year later the Professor was in her study, reading about a magnificent Moorish pendant that was being offered for sale. The guard who watched over the storage vault burst in.

"Professor, the vault has been robbed! So far it appears that only a few things were taken—the fibula, a Vandal bracelet for certain. I cannot tell you . . . I have been so careful . . ." the guard spluttered in fear and misery. She stood trembling at attention, awaiting Doña Ternilla's wrath.

But what was this? The guard could not believe her eyes. Tears were rolling down the Professor's cheeks and her face was shining with a radiant smile.

Metal

JAE LIVED NEAR A TOWN which, though small, had a number of famous schools. She had always wanted to study jewelry-making but her family was poor and could not help her. She pursued her goal with steadfast determination. Eventually she received a scholarship to the town's prestigious school of jewelry design. Everyone at the school was impressed with her diligence, skill, and original ideas.

After learning the properties of various metals, she was given pure silver for her first projects. A short time later she was advanced to gold. She then received a great honor: she was chosen to work in platinum. Only one student each year was selected to work with this rare metal. Other students were envious, yet also happy for her. Her family beamed with pride.

Jae was troubled. She was bored and dissatisfied with the jewelry she made. She went to the office of the headmistress and knocked on the door.

"Come in." When the headmistress saw who it was, her face lit up. "Jae, what can I do for you?"

"I do not want to work with platinum."

"Don't be afraid, my dear," was the kindly reply.

Metal

"It's natural to feel daunted when you begin."

"I am not afraid."

"Well," reflected the headmistress, "since you are unhappy, would you prefer to remain with gold?"

"No, I do not want to work in gold, either."

"Not gold? But you made such fine pieces. You won awards. Already people want to commission you." The headmistress sighed. "So it's silver. I'm disappointed. Even the untalented students work in silver."

"No, I do not want to work in silver, either."

The headmistress shook her head. "I'm quite surprised. We were all so sure of your commitment to jewelry-making. What has changed your mind?"

"I do not want to give up jewelry-making."

The head of the school was losing patience. "What is it, then? What do you want?"

"I want to work with tin."

"Tin! That is crazy! Tin is cheap and ugly! No one will buy it!" shouted the headmistress.

"But that is what I want to do."

"I'm not at all pleased. You were our most promising student. And now you're throwing away everything you have learned." The headmistress practically shoved Jae out of her office and slammed the door.

When the students learned what had happened, they

were shocked. "Not silver, not gold, not plat-in-um, it's tin, tin, tin," they chanted.

Jae lost her scholarship and had to leave the school. Her family was overcome with shame. They threw her out of the house.

The poorest of the poor lived in shacks at the garbage dump and foraged in the debris. Jae, having nowhere else to go, wandered into the dump. The air was gray and acrid from many small fires. Several scavengers were bent over, poking through the rubble. Jae saw mounds and mounds of glass and paper and rags and tin cans.

Her heart beat fast with happiness. "This is perfect," she said to herself.

The Feast on the Plain

THE FOLLOWING IS A NEW TRANSLATION of the so-called
Feast Manuscript, widely considered to be the most sig-
nificant of the Ciquaymal Caves cloth texts. It has been
dated to the Joro period, near the end of the Decline. It
is thought to be one of the most representative narra-
tives of Xychlea culture, transmitted orally for several
generations prior to the creation of the manuscript.

The landscape is a desolate plain. It was once a forest,
long since felled. Toward evening there are brilliant
red sunsets. Vegetation is sparse; here and there a
ravaged bush endures. The desiccated carcasses of
liyuna (a type of ground squirrel) are scattered on the
cracked earth.

A group of noblewomen have decided to hold a
feast on the plain. This is partly for the pleasure of
novelty and partly for safety. A large gathering inside
a dwelling would be risky now. Too many nobles are
being killed in their homes, despite bodyguards.

A long table is set out on the hard ground. The
finest pottery, jeweled cutlery, and weavings are placed
on the table. Soldiers surround the table and the area

189

nearby where the food is prepared. The food is brought to the table under guard.

The evening sky is fiery. The noblewomen gather.

As the dinner proceeds, the poor appear, seemingly from nowhere. The soldiers motion them away but they remain and beg for food. The guards have their weapons ready. The noblewomen continue to eat. The hungry crowd increases.

Though the circle of guards is strong, there is the thought, "What if one of them allowed the ring to be broken?"

It is impossible and then it happens: the surging crowd finds a weakness in the phalanx. Someone breaks through and rushes toward the table. It is a pregnant woman. A soldier was not forceful enough with her. The woman must be stopped or the crowd will follow. A noblewoman rises up in fear and opens her mouth as if she is about to say something.

A scream begins and is cut short. The soldier next to the weak one has slain the intruding woman with a sword. The crowd grows quiet and stops pushing toward the table.

The noblewoman sits down. The feast resumes. The ring of guards closes again. The weak guard is stripped of her weapon and forced into the crowd.

The slain woman lies bleeding next to the table. One of the dinner guests looks over at her. With shock she recognizes the woman: she was a friend who lost her fortune a short time ago.

Fat steaming *gargya* (a domesticated fowl) are brought to the table. The crowd, wild with the smell of the savory birds, surges forward. The nobles' hands and forearms are soon covered in succulent fat. There is clubbing now, of the more persistent poor. Before the night is over, swords will be brandished again.

Jumping

WE ARE TRANSFIXED BY THE SITUATION. The woman is so high up, just a speck. And then, thinking about how far down it is to the street, just to look almost pushes us off the ledge. The faintest breeze might blow us over. Later, thinking about it at home in the evening, we are in danger of falling out of our chairs.

The crowd is yelling, "Jump, jump!" We are in that crowd whose soul hovers so far above us. We yell, too. Our throats hurt.

Were you there? The despairing woman can hear her heartbeat. She is thinking about how she will be missed by her friends and good-for-nothing boss. This will show them. How unhappy she is!

What is that sound coming up from the street? She looks down. A hundred tiny dots. What are they saying? "Ump ump jump jump." They are shouting for me to jump!

In a flash she understands: her friends and boss are hoping for it! Their entreaties and tears are all a sham. Now her only fear is that she will slip. Never has she known such terror as when she edges back toward the window.

192

Didn't we in our wisdom know what to do? The speck is moving back to the window. We are silent. Our hearts stop beating. "Let her not fall," we pray. Never have we been so relieved as when she disappears into the open window.

The newspaper reporter is half a block away. She hears the chanting of the crowd. What is it? She looks up: a woman on the ledge! And the crowd shouting! A much better story than the one she was about to write. She is late and must rush off. It does not occur to her that her story will be retold, will become legend and a proof of many things.

There are a number of such stories. Every one we have looked into so far has been false.

Love and Peace

ON A SULTRY AFTERNOON HON was sitting outside, cataloging texts on the library terrace. A renowned commercial traveler came running toward her. "I must talk to you at once," she gasped.

"Of course. Please sit down."

Immediately the two women were deep in conversation. After awhile Hon called over to her assistant. "Send a messenger to the senators. They are to be summoned to an emergency session tonight; it is regarding Imia." The assistant nodded and dashed from the terrace.

Hon turned back to the visitor. "I want you to tell them what you have just told me."

"I will," said the traveler. She departed and Hon returned to her catalogues.

At workday's end Hon set out toward home. She was starting up the steps to her house when there was a blur in the fading light. Yar, her little dog, leapt into her arms, yipping with pleasure.

The librarian cried out, "My heart, my joy, my precious one," as Yar licked her face and hands, its small body quivering with devotion. Hon buried her nose in the warm spiky fur at the back of the little dog's neck and inhaled deeply. The familiar scent filled her with well-being. No returning hero, no prodigal, no one thought dead, could have been more gladly received; no reunion could have been more heartfelt than this, between Hon and Yar, after a separation of a few hours. Nor was it a unique scene: everywhere in the land the women were coming home from work and greeting their beloved little dogs.

The country flourished in every endeavor: commerce, industry, engineering, science, the arts, law, and diplomacy. On all sides shone examples of what could be achieved when discourse was clear, when everyone worked together for the common weal, with allowances made for individual opinion and taste.

Later, in the moonlight, the senators made their way to the *curia*. The meeting was called to order by the *praeses* and the traveler was recognized.

"Senators, I bring grave news. The nation of Imia continues its path of conquest. Country after country has given way to its fearsome weapons, brilliant battle plans, and implacable ambition. I have witnessed the wake of its battles: heartache and devastation. The Imian army spares nothing. Once I was within sight of a skirmish and observed these soldiers. Each of them displayed a fearlessness and ferocity I have never witnessed before.

"If you think you have leisure to plan a defense, you are mistaken. Your neighbor, the last country that still buffers you, is armed and ready. But I would not count on its being victorious. I fear it will succumb like all the others. The Imians will be at your border sooner than you expect. You must prepare yourselves now."

Next, Hon, the senate's most respected member, was recognized. "There is cause for concern but not alarm. Peace has prevailed in our land for as long as can be remembered. Diplomacy is widely acknowledged to be our greatest achievement; a solution will be found. I have an idea, but first I would like to hear from the rest of you."

The chief engineer, one of the newest senators, spoke next. "Perhaps we should build some sort of wall, or fortress ourselves in some way. I will need a bit more time to—"

A physician interrupted. "But we have no military. Are we to await our slaughter while we sit quietly behind a wall? It's time to arm ourselves. Past time. We must begin at once."

The discussion ranged on.

Finally Hon spoke again. "My proposal is this: we produce a spectacle for the Imian troops, one which possesses such compelling poetry, such exquisite music and dancing, that the soldiers will weep and be moved to lay down their arms. Furthermore, I suggest that scouts be dispatched immediately, to infiltrate the army in order to learn the Imian language and customs."

A vote was taken and Hon's proposal was carried. Scouts were sent out that very night. Soon, information was arriving for incorporation into the spectacle. At the border where the Imians were most likely to enter, construction of a huge stage began. An epic play was started, costumes were sewn, sets were built, music was composed and rehearsed, actors studied their lines and dancers perfected their turns.

From a mountain lookout, enemy troops were sighted on the horizon. The neighboring country's last fortressed city stood between the army and the women's land. Already the smell of battle could be detected, at least by those with keen senses.

The little dogs were pacing and staying awake at night. They were running to their mistresses and whining for food and water. The women attempted to give increased attention to their dear ones, even in the midst of the urgent preparations for the spectacle. But their little dogs could not be placated.

Hon said to Yar, "My darling, aren't you growing just a little stouter? Of course you are as beautiful as ever, but this constant begging for food, which you know I cannot refuse you, could make you ill." In response, Yar licked its mistress's face and implored her for a treat.

A few days later, Hon and Yar had another colloquy. "Dearest, it seems that treats are no longer enough. You yelp and yelp unless I give you substantial meals several times a day. I know you are worried about the army. But I would never let anyone harm you." After which Yar dashed into the kitchen and whined loudly for another dinner.

Yar started digging up the vegetable garden and ripping into bags of food. Perhaps Hon did not devote as much attention to these matters as she should have. She merely carried on with her usual good-natured tolerance.

Not long afterwards, Hon was again attempting to calm her little dog with food and endearments. Suddenly Yar scampered down the hill. A pack of dogs was passing by. "Yar! Come back!" pleaded Hon, but the little dog paid no heed and ran off with the pack.

Hon visited the stage site the next day. Many of the women were saying that their little dogs had formed roaming packs. Furthermore, the packs were causing widespread damage: uprooting crops and breaking into storage sheds. While they were talking, a distraught woman ran up to them, shouting, "A pack of little dogs has attacked a flock of sheep and torn them to pieces!"

Another emergency senate meeting was convened. That evening as a senator was speaking, a pack burst into the chamber. They barked and ran on the tables, upsetting water pitchers and trampling papers. The meeting was adjourned in confusion.

Wearily, the senators arrived for a session the following night. The topic was the little dogs again, and what was to be done.

The physician rose and said, "I believe the behavior of the little dogs should be viewed as a portent. We are underestimating the danger of our situation and the dogs are doing their best to warn us. We have never developed military might. It is time to do so."

Hon responded, "We have not developed military might because we have maintained the longest peace ever enjoyed by any nation. Our diplomatic methods have proven successful time and again. Let us not be diverted by the actions of our wayward pets. Let us continue to assure them of our constancy and devotion. Soon enough, I am confident, this latest threat to our peace will be resolved and our loving little dogs will come back to us."

The session continued far into the night. No consensus was reached. The interim plan was that the women would continue to manage their little dogs as best they could.

The problem was intensifying: packs were destroying the reserve food supplies. The devouring of food was so widespread there was a possibility of famine.

The women faced an unprecedented crisis: a mighty enemy nearing their border and a wild element undermining domestic stability from within. Hurried measures to control the dogs were undertaken: emergency obedience schools with massive rewards and fairly severe punishments; containment behind strong fences. But even when the dogs were successfully impounded, they soon knocked down the fences and roamed free again. Still, in all their misbehavior, there was no incident of a dog attacking a woman.

Periodically Hon would see Yar in the distance as it traveled with its pack. One day Yar left the pack and ran over to her. It looked up with pleading eyes, as if to say, Don't you see my loyalty? Don't you know that everything I do is for you?

"Oh, Yar, how I wish I could hold you in my arms again. There is nothing to fear. Try to calm yourself."

Yar raced off toward the border and back again, barking and looking back and forth between Hon and the army's path of approach, as if to sound the alert that the enemy was at their very gates.

It was true. The neighbor's city lay in ruins. Smoke hung solidly at the border and drifted in ugly streaks across the land. The enemy was near and coming nearer.

It was time for the spectacle. The women gathered at the site, hungry and exhausted. The performers pulled themselves up the ladders to the stage.

Trumpets sounded the opening fanfare as the army crossed into the land. The first actors appeared. The play began with a paean to peace in the Imian language.

The enemy stopped in confusion and amazement. Seeing no sign of confrontation, fascinated at hearing their language spoken with such skill, they surged toward the stage. The chorus emerged and began an exquisite song. The dancers glided forward. The soldiers sat down as one, spellbound. A few moments later, tears began to run down their cheeks. They dropped their weapons.

Then the ground began to shake. The entire population of little dogs, now huge, leapt over the stage and headed for the army, barking wildly. The soldiers sprang up, seizing their weapons. The women cried out for the little dogs to come back, but their voices were drowned by the din. They watched in horror as the dogs attacked the foe: some soldiers were torn to shreds, some dogs were brutally slaughtered.

The women retreated. They formed a crowd around the *curia* while the senators hastened inside. The *praeses* called the meeting to order and asked Hon for her comments.

Hon stood. She was pale and trembling. "I am shocked by what has occurred. I was so certain the spectacle would succeed. But I was blind to what was happening to our little dogs. I confess I have no remedy to offer. I only hope that someone has a clearer mind than I." She sat down and bowed her head in sorrow and defeat.

Senator after senator rose and admitted to confusion and helplessness. Yelps and shrieks could be heard in the distance.

One thought hung heaviest in the woeful air: the halcyon age of peace was at an end.

The Old Composer

THE TOWN OF N—— IS FAR to the north. Winters are dark and cold; summers, though the days are long, are overcast and dreary. Our buildings are drab. The people, too, are in general rather colorless. There is an exception, however, which stands out in contrast to the town's culture of melancholy indifference: our symphony orchestra.

The N—— Philharmonic Orchestra, while an unpaid group, is a powerful and successful institution. Currently we have fifty-one members. Every year aspiring musicians audition; very few are chosen.

Peert, our conductor, is highly talented, with perfect pitch and an impressive repertoire of memorized scores of the great classical symphonies. Her only fault is a touch of deafness. She tends to conduct everything forte and above. Yet even this quirk has its advantages: our audience seems to particularly enjoy her rousing interpretations.

Our winter concert series attracts almost all the townspeople; they brave winter storms and gloom in order to hear music that sometimes borders on the sublime. We rehearse for three hours every weekday in the old community center which smells of floor-wax and buzzes from the flickering lights overhead.

One icy Tuesday at rehearsal, everyone was tuning up as usual, to me, the only oboe. Second Trumpet was having trouble with her tuning slide and cursing softly. Peert was on her podium, flexing her hands to warm up. An old woman, a stranger, shuffled in. This was unusual; outsiders are rare in N——. Furthermore, Peert discourages visitors.

Everything about the woman was worn-out: her shapeless coat, deflated hat, and ancient briefcase. She waited beside the podium while the orchestra finished tuning.

We sat at attention, whispering beneath the limit of Peert's hearing. First Flute hissed, "Who is that sad-looking soul?"

"You should know," responded Second Cello Third Chair, "she looks like a flutist."

The visitor looked at Peert and pointed to her brief-case. The conductor nodded curtly. The old woman took out a score and handed it to Peert, who started to put it aside. The old woman shook her head.

Everyone was amazed when Peert opened the score and glanced at it, then went back to the beginning and examined it page by page. The old woman reached into the briefcase and removed a thick stack of papers. Peert took it and called out, "Flutes and piccolos! Violins! Viola! Cellos! Basses! Woodwinds! French horns and brasses! Percussion!" as she handed out our parts.

I eagerly looked mine over, curious as to what could have induced Peert to veer from her protocol. The piece looked difficult and more modern than was customary for us.

Peert nodded to the woman to dismiss her. The old woman shook her head. The conductor ignored her and called out the first selection of the day. She raised her baton and we began.

Then the old woman did something unthinkable: she stepped up onto the podium and tapped Peert on the arm. The conductor stopped in disbelief and we ground musically to a halt.

The woman rasped out, "When?"

Peert impatiently waved her hand. "One week."

Finally the old woman walked out. The baton went up and we resumed.

That night after dinner I put the new piece, Symphony Number One, on my music stand and started practicing. The part was unusual: pages of staccato notes in constantly shifting time signatures. Sometimes

I entered on the beat, sometimes before or after. A few hours later I felt I had mastered it. I wondered how the others were faring.

For the rest of the week, Symphony Number One was the subject of our excited whispers. Everyone was practicing and discussing what it would sound like when we were all playing it together.

I worked on it every evening. I decided to memorize it, since I would have to watch Peert closely in order to follow the changing meters and tempos.

Over the weekend First Flute was particularly harsh: her Saturday and Sunday section rehearsals lasted far into the night. On Monday the French horns had swollen red lips from long hours of struggle.

It was another cold dark Tuesday. The old composer was there when we arrived, unchanged except for her eyes: they burned with a new fervor.

The orchestra tuned. Peert announced, "Symphony Number One." The old composer walked to the center of the auditorium. The conductor raised her baton and brought it down.

It was fortunate I had memorized my part: the changes were dizzying. We followed Peert like thoroughbreds, responding instantly to changes of tempo, meter and dynamic. The piece charged on without recapitulation or respite. It leapt from complexity to complexity, always unpredictable, until unpredictability itself became a certainty, curiously satisfying.

Flutes and piccolos were a precision regiment; strings moved back and forth between pizzicato and bowing at breakneck speed; woodwinds were a kaleidoscope of staccato geometries; French horns jumped between octaves, hitting their notes; brasses frantically emptied their spit valves; percussionists raced among their instruments.

Never had the orchestra been so focused, never had we played with such daring and virtuosity.

The piece gathered itself for the finale, the tempo so fast the various notes fused in the ear in a complex glissando: the treble parts rising like skyrockets, the basses crashing down like meteors. With a final sforzando it was over.

We had triumphed.

I was breathless with exhilaration. I almost expected thunderous applause. The buzzing lights were the only sound. The old composer walked toward us, her eyes shining, the hint of a smile on her face.

First Flute eventually cleared her throat: "I'm not sure you understand the register of the flute. Some of these notes are almost impossible to play."

Second Cello Third Chair followed: "The flute, always complaining. Don't bother listening to her. But pizzicato on the cello was not meant to be done so rapidly. One cannot get a full, rich sound."

First Violin First Chair, our concertmistress, made her contribution: "The violin is a haunting instrument. Its strength is its lyricism. Your symphony has none of that. You would do well to include some slower, more reflective passages, to allow for the beauty of the instrument to shine through."

Second Trumpet weighed in: "The string players are getting carried away, as usual. But speaking for the brasses, we scarcely had time to breathe or empty our spit valves and slides. Your symphony will never be successful unless you pay attention to the needs of the musicians. I don't want to play in front of an audience and have my horn so full of saliva I can't produce a clear note."

I thought I should add something: "As the only oboe, I must concur with what the others have said. Every instrument has its special quality, yet your piece does not take advantage of these attributes. The tonality of the oboe lends itself to sensuality, like earth and new wood. But the notes you have given me sound more like a calliope."

Finally Peert spoke: "Thank you for showing us your interesting composition. It is important that the conductor have an understanding of each work that is performed. I stand before the audience and bear the responsibility for every piece. There are moments in your symphony I think I understand. But just as a moment comes, it moves to something else. Your work is too jumpy, too nervous. You must slow it down. It is needlessly complicated; you must simplify it. Listen to the great masters. See how they take a theme and develop it gradually, so that the listeners—and the performers, too—have time to take it in, and to enjoy it."

As the old composer listened to us, her eyes ceased to sparkle. If possible, she looked even older and shabbier. She said nothing, neither thanking us nor commenting on our suggestions. This struck me as thoughtless, given our hard work.

Peert turned to us and said, "Hand back your parts." She gave them to the old composer, who returned them to her briefcase and walked out the door.

I heard her footsteps receding down the hallway. A few moments later they were drowned out by the buzzing of the lights.

The Farmer

A FARMER, JEY, SOWED HER FIELDS. They brought forth grain but she did not gather her crop; planting was what she loved, not harvesting. The following year she sowed again. In between, the decaying, unharvested grain fertilized the land. The next crop was even better, and thus it went for several years.

People said, "How wasteful. You sow and sow, and your crop flourishes. But if you do not reap, what is the use?"

Finally, she grew so tired of listening to everyone's carping that she harvested her crop. The grain was put into a silo. Every year more silos filled with grain.

People said, "How wasteful. You reap and reap, and silo after silo fills with grain. But if you do not sell it, what is the use?"

Weary of the complaints, she found a buyer for her grain.

"At last you are a real farmer," people told her.

But she knew she had always been a real farmer—when she harvested, and before that, when she sowed. And even before that, when she felt her love for planting and dreamed of it at night.

The Lion Tamer

ONE AFTERNOON A LARGE BUT SECOND-RATE circus came
to town. It was earliest spring: the sky throbbed with
veiled light, the thawed grass lay flat and pale. From
afar, Finst watched as a long procession of wagons
crawled onto a barren patch of ground. Later a huge
tent fluttered heavily upward.

She suddenly remembered an acquaintance, who,
when last she heard, was going off to work as a lion
tamer with this very outfit. She walked over to the
tent and asked for directions, then proceeded through
a bustling warren of wagons and performers to the
perimeter, where the trainers were exercising their animals. Off by itself was a crude structure of close-set
poles bound together with wire, covered at the top by
a dirty white canvas.

Owwrrllh! An unearthly howl flew through the
air. Peering between the poles, Finst recognized her
old friend and, on a high striped stand, a lumpish
shaggy thing.

"Hinje! Hallo!"

After a pause the lion tamer called back curtly, "Yes,
I see you."

"May I come inside the cage?"

"Too dangerous."

"I'll do exactly as you say."

"I'm busy now."

" Just tell me what to do and I'll obey."

"Quiet. You're disturbing the animal."

"I'll be silent as soon as you let me inside."

Irritably, Hinje unlocked the cage door, keeping her eyes on the lump all the while. "Walk slowly and stand over there. Then be still and don't say a word."

Inside, the light was filtered and shadowless. The ground was covered with a worn tarp, the stand was chipped and scarred. Finst was disappointed to see that the object on the stand was a pathetic specimen of a lion with a patchy, moth-eaten coat, and a quailing, skulking manner. Whereas Hinje, who had always been tall and strapping, radiated the very peak of health.

"Back! Hiyy!" The tamer shouted commands and flourished a long whip which shrieked through the air and snapped loudly against the stand. As soon as the whip began to scream, the wretched creature flinched, then listlessly performed its next stunt.

Aaoowrrllh! The animal made a little slip on the stand. Immediately the lash struck its bony leg, which was drawn back quickly with a wrenching wail.

Finst could not help herself. "Why are you so brutal with that poor old thing? Attacking it the way you do, how cruel!" She almost never criticized anyone; on the rare occasions when she did, she hastened to recant and apologize. But watching Hinje and the lion, she was so upset that she stood with her jaw thrust forward, her eyes unblinking.

The tamer shouted, "Hayy! Hiyy!" paying no attention to Finst's comments.

"Let me out," demanded Finst, feeling helpless and disgusted.

"As you wish." Hinje unlocked the cage with a look of bemused superiority.

A week later the circus was nearing the end of its stay. Finst was beginning to think she had been too severe with her friend. After all, hadn't the tamer been working with that grizzled old animal for years? And doesn't it happen that when one is continuously involved with another, one becomes blind to the changes that are taking place? It's the outsider who has the advantage of fresh appraisal.

She went back to the circus and found Hinje in the cage, putting the lion through its paces.

"Hallo, may I come into the cage again?"

Hinje unlocked the door without comment. Finst entered and went to her post. She was determined to reconcile at the first opportunity. The creature looked even more miserable than before and another patch of fur was gone.

Eeeeyrtt! The whip screeched and snapped.

Despite her resolve, Finst's distress and anger returned. "Hinje," she said, as calmly as she could, "I'm concerned about your lion. It's growing more feeble with every passing week. Surely you needn't strike at it as if it were still young and strong."

"You simply don't understand." In response to some misstep, the whip sizzled through the air and caught the lion on a toe.

Owwrm owwrm owwrm, the lion whimpered, drawing back its paw.

"Hiyy! This lion may look harmless, but I assure you, it's strong enough to tear my—or your—arm off in an instant."

Finst was unable to let go of the matter. Some sense of horror was aroused in her, as if it were her own flesh that was being struck. "I think you've been working with that animal for so long, you don't see how weak it has become."

"You know nothing about it."

214

"But perhaps I do. I've been watching closely."

"It's not as simple as it seems."

Eeeeyrtt! All the while the whip was flying.

Finst groaned. She felt sick to her stomach.

"Believe me, a few minutes in a cage does not make you a lion tamer," said Hinje.

"Just once," Finst persisted, "couldn't you just shake the whip and see if your friend doesn't respond as you desire?"

"Enough," growled the tamer. "Alright. But first you have to leave the cage. I won't put you in danger."

"I want to stay. This is my idea. I'm entirely confident."

"Once, then. If you will stop talking."

"Heeiiy!" commanded the tamer. Then, with perfect control, she cast the whip through the air, but gently, so that it made a pleasing musical sound.

The lion started to cringe, but upon hearing the new sound, it stopped in midmotion, a look of wonderment on its haggard face. Suddenly it lunged toward Hinje, knocked her down, and thrust its teeth deep into the hand that held the whip. The tamer screamed as the whip fell.

Finst grabbed the lash and struck. A few drops of blood sprang from the monster's exposed hide.

The depraved animal looked at Finst in surprise and pulled its teeth out of the tamer.

Finst struck again.

Owwwrrrlllh!! Clumsily, the savage clambered up onto its perch.

"Damn you, damn you, damn you!" Finst could not stop shouting, could not stop slashing at the evil beast.

The tamer managed to stand. She lurched toward Finst and tried to snatch away the whip; Finst would not let go.

The creature collapsed and fell but the flailing went on. Hinje hurled herself at Finst, pulled her to the ground, and seized the whip.

They were all in the red blood on the floor: the beast crumpled in a heap; Finst, breathing harshly, returning from a wilderness within herself she had never suspected; and the lion tamer, bleeding from one hand, grasping the whip in the other.

The Headmistress

FLUR CAME FROM A LONG LINE of teachers. All of them loved three things: learning, march music, and patriotism.

The most thrilling event in her life was a school trip to the nation's capital when she was in third grade. On a brilliant cold morning she had stood in the throng as a parade of soldiers marched past. A band was playing—the bass drum was pounding like her young heart, the trumpets blared like beautiful harsh birds. At that moment her future was revealed: she would become a teacher and lead young minds to such wonders.

She attended a teachers' college. While there she met others who were also descended from generations of teachers. At night, walking across the campus from the library, they confided their aspirations, laughing in the icy air.

Flur got her credential and began her first job: teaching third grade. In the fall, keeping up with her lesson plans took all of her time. But in the spring she was able to organize a field trip to see a parade.

Most of the class went on the trip. They all stood in

the parade viewing area roped off for school children.

Flur's heart beat hard when she heard the drums; it soared when she heard the trumpets. Here came the waving flags, here came the soldiers. She looked over at her students, beaming.

The next day she led the class in a discussion of the trip. None of the students found it particularly interesting.

Later, Flur became a headmistress. The young minds she had dreamed of leading turned out to be only one, her own. There was no one else.

Among Volcanoes

IT WAS THE MOST TREACHEROUS part of the voyage.
We had left Borneo and were on the trade route
through the Sunda Strait. Old Perboewatan and
Danan had been grumbling from time to time; we
were praying to get through without incident.

Then this morning, the loudest explosion imaginable, like the world breaking in half. Later, ash rained
down and the sky turned black. Waves and wind ran
this way and that. We quaked in our souls as we listened to the thunder booms and felt our vessel tremble
from the unnatural waves' roundhouse blows.

We needed to haul out as fast as possible. Instead
we were drifting. Just before all light was extinguished,
we saw our captain beating the mate Coolin with a
savagery as merciless as the elements. Had we been
brave we would have intevened. But we ran the other
way—to the saloon, our place of comfort on good days,
of necessity on this harrowing false night. The captain never ventured here. She spent her days and nights
pacing alone.

We locked the door behind us. Someone seized a
rum bottle and poured tumblerfuls all round. The

lanterns were shivering and swinging in wide arcs, but their warm light and the quickening rum infused an aliquot of cheer.

"Perhaps Coolin is dead," someone whispered.

We heard a new sound in the din. Was someone knocking on the saloon door? Outside was the wild captain and poor Coolin with her unnamed crime. No one moved. In our fear and shame we all began whispering at once. The passenger Vey had been silent and aloof during the voyage. Now she spoke; her voice held a tone of urgent authority which caused the rest of us to fall silent.

"Permit me to explain certain matters to you," she began. "Riye and Blaiz were sisters. Blaiz, the older, was unusually virtuous: kind and generous, with a passion for justice. Everyone who knew her felt inspired toward love and admiration. The younger sister, Riye, who is our captain, worshipped her. As a result of her sister's influence, Riye became a seminarian, planning to become a missionary.

"Though Blaiz avoided bringing harm to any living thing, when the war came she embraced the cause and enlisted as a foot soldier. Her company was made up of rough women. Blaiz was soon the unspoken leader, admired and loved, as always happened.

"One soldier, Teece, was thought to be untrustworthy and something of a shirker. Blaiz befriended the outcast but the rest of the company kept their distance.

"During a fierce encounter with the enemy, Teece did a cowardly and reprehensible thing: panicking when her rifle jammed, she crept up behind one of her comrades, struck her, and seized her weapon. The other soldier, fallen and defenseless, was soon killed.

"Later in the day, Teece, on some pretext, asked to exchange rifles with Blaiz. When an accounting was made of the day's actions, Teece related the incident of the stolen gun but blamed it on Blaiz. Blaiz had the dead soldier's rifle in her possession; it was damning evidence. Yet had Blaiz spoken up, she would have been believed, for she was trusted and beloved and Teece was not. But Blaiz sat mutely, almost in a trance. She was court-martialed and sent to prison.

"Even in prison Blaiz felt no anger toward Teece. She blamed herself, though she could not explain why. A few months later Blaiz received a letter from the craven soldier. In it, Teece asked for a favor: she asked Blaiz to lie on her behalf, in order to protect her from another criminal prosecution. Amazingly, Blaiz complied."

Vey paused and swallowed a mouthful of rum. "You may be wondering how I know these things: I was in the cell next to Blaiz. Over time I learned her story. My own crime I shall not disclose; suffice it to say, I have paid for it in full.

"Riye often visited at the prison. She begged her sister to tell her what had happened, but Blaiz would not. Riye was so upset by the imprisonment, I eventually took it upon myself to go to the visitors' room and speak to her. I told her the truth. On hearing it, Riye pleaded with Blaiz to vindicate herself, but her efforts were in vain.

"After that, Riye was changed. She wouldn't allow anyone to cross her, not even in the smallest way. Whoever tried regretted it. She left the seminary and went to sea. By dint of fierce determination she worked her way up until she became a ship's captain."

Vey stopped and emptied her glass. The vessel pitched sharply.

Someone blurted out, "Let's go." We all sprang up and ran to the door. When we opened it, Coolin fell inside, bloodied but alive. We stepped over her and rushed headlong into the smothering darkness.

The Oxcart Wheel

THE POET LI FAN RARELY TRAVELED on the narrow
road through the mountains, certainly not in the rainy
season. But she had won a prize and was to receive
it in the capital, then give a lecture. She secured a
bundle of supplies under the seat of her oxcart, hitched
up her ox, and crying out, "Hu!" set forth on the treacherous pass. Rain fell relentlessly; the road was slippery
and deserted.

She had been traveling awhile when she saw, dim-
ly, an odd shape in the road. As she came nearer she
discerned that it was an oxcart, all awry. One of its
huge wheels had broken apart; one side of the cart
dipped down low while the other side stuck up high
in the air. The poor driver was standing next to the
cart, distractedly talking to her ox. When she saw the
poet, she cried out, "Oh, help us!"

Fan had far to go and night was coming but she
said, "I will try."

The two women looked at the broken wheel. It was
so old, one of its spokes had splintered, the rim had
sprung off, and the whole wheel had come partway
off its axle.

Fan saw a grove of young trees a short distance below the road. "Let's get some sapling wood," she said. The women climbed down to the grove, slipping and falling on the muddy slope. Fan had a sharp knife and the two women managed to cut down a young tree. The poet whittled a spoke from it. She grooved one end and fitted it onto the hub. The women pushed the sprung rim back into place and secured it several times with rope Li Fan had in her wagon. They positioned the oxen to push the wheel back onto the axle: one ox pushed the wheel with its shoulder while the other stood on the opposite side of the wagon and steadied the cart against its flank.

The woman, a farmer named Na Ming, was almost weeping with gratitude. "I don't know what would have happened to me without your help."

"That's the way it is in the mountains," said Fan. "Travelers must help each other. Perhaps one day I will be the one with the broken wheel."

They hitched their oxen and were about to head off in opposite directions. Just then a woman came along on foot.

"I saw what happened," she said.

Ming called out to her, "Since you are going in my direction, come up into my cart. I will take you a ways."

Fan traveled all night. At times she had to get down and crawl on the ground, feeling with her hands for the turns in the road. As it grew lighter, making progress was easier. She was only a little delayed in reaching the capital. She received her prize and gave her lecture.

The next morning she set out on the pass to return. It was still raining; this time the road was completely deserted.

When she got home, it was evening. As she was unhitching her ox in the muddy stable-yard, someone came rushing toward her, shouting, "How dare you presume to fix a broken wheel! Are you a wheelwright? And how dare you presume to force oxen to push here and stand there! Are you an ox trainer?"

It was the walking woman from the mountain road. Fan felt sorry for her. "I am not a wheelwright and I am not an ox trainer. But travelers must help each other if no one else is around. Na Ming and I did the best we could under the circumstances."

When she finished speaking, the walking woman repeated her angry words and added, "I am going to bring the matter up at the village council."

Fan was exhausted but she explained a second time, speaking more slowly.

The walking woman made her accusations a third time, then departed. Fan fed her ox and went into the house. She changed into dry clothes and went to sleep.

She was awakened by the sound of voices in the stable-yard. "Li Fan! Li Fan! You must come to the council meeting!" She dragged herself out of bed and went to the council-house.

The chief turned her head toward Li Fan and said, "We need you to explain certain things that are said to have taken place on the mountain road, concerning a wheel and some oxen."

"I will be happy—" began Li Fan.

The walking woman interrupted, widening her eyes and baring her teeth at the poet, shouting, "I saw it all. This woman deliberately drove the other woman off the road. Then she tried to steal her ox. I came along and helped the other poor woman to escape." She turned to Li Fan. "You know what you did. You might as well confess."

Fan could hardly believe what was happening. She tried to speak again. "It began—"

But the walking woman interrupted and repeated her story.

Fan was having a difficult time keeping her eyes open. She said, "Perhaps the matter can best be settled by bringing in the other party. Her name is Na Ming."

"An excellent idea," said the chief.

"Now we will get to the truth of the matter," said the walking woman.

Fan lay down in a corner and went to sleep.

When Na Ming was brought in, Fan was awakened. The chief asked Ming to give her version of events.

"With pleasure," said Ming. "This woman, Li Fan, saved me. I was returning from the city on the road through the mountains, in pouring rain, when my oxcart wheel broke. Li Fan was kind, generous, and resourceful. Together we fixed the wheel so that I could get home. I also gave a ride to this other woman, whose name I do not know."

"Did Li Fan cause you to run off the road?"

"I didn't go off the road. My wheel was so old it broke down of its own accord."

"Did Li Fan try to steal your ox?"

"Of course not. That is ridiculous."

"Did Li Fan force you to pay her a great deal of money in return for her help?"

"She asked for nothing. She merely said, 'Perhaps one day I will be the one with the broken wheel.'"

"Thank you," said the chief. "Li Fan, you are free to go."

The walking woman had been growing more and more agitated. Now she exploded. "Both women are lying! I was there! Li Fan must have threatened to harm Na Ming if she told the truth!"

"That is as may be," said the chief, "but since the supposed injured party makes no complaint, no further action is required."

Fan thanked Ming. Then she went home, crawled back into bed, and slept. She woke up feeling troubled. "I am tired," she said to herself. "When I am rested, this will be behind me." But she was still thinking about the incident several days later. She felt vaguely afraid.

In the village the walking woman kept up her accusations. It was an occasion for the villagers to speculate and gossip. Though most felt that Li Fan was probably blameless, still, they wondered what was causing the walking woman to continue her attack.

Fan was in her stable-yard. The mud was beginning to dry and she was doing some sweeping.

Some villagers were passing by. "Hello, Li Fan," they called out.

Fan was not sure, but she thought she detected a hint of malice or mockery—or perhaps inquisitiveness—in their greetings. She now felt suspicious whenever she saw anyone.

Eventually the walking woman left the village. Nothing ever came of the matter of the oxcart wheel.

Quite some time has passed since then, but so far Li Fan has not been able to write a single word of poetry.

Sand

SEVERAL AREAS OF THE COUNTRY were so impenetrable they had never been mapped, or even seen. The government hired the famous explorer, Raiy, to go into these areas. One of the things Raiy discovered was a lake with a beautiful beach of the purest white sand. The government gave her the beach in perpetuity, to honor her outstanding contributions.

Later, a community developed by the lake. Raiy was generous with her beach and allowed anyone to use it.

Her friend, the writer Jae, moved to the lake community. She loved the beach and walked there often. Raiy made sure that Jae could always visit the beach: she put it in her will. Then she died.

Raiy's heirs closed the beach to the public. Jae, however, continued her beach walks. The heirs were not happy about it but there was nothing they could do.

One day Jae was working at her desk. She was distracted by the feel of something in her shoes. She took them off and found several grains of sand inside. She was about to dump the sand in the wastebasket; instead, thinking of Raiy, she placed the grains on a saucer.

Jae was writing her memoirs. A well-known artist

was commissioned to do a portrait for the book. She painted a fine picture of the writer at her desk.

Raiy's heirs learned of Jae's forthcoming book. Curious as to what Jae might say about their relative, they asked to see the book before it was released. They read it carefully and found several references to Raiy, including a brief mention of the sand in the saucer. A sharp-eyed heir, on examining the portrait, noticed something that looked like particles in a saucer on the writer's desk.

The heirs and their lawyers went to court. They wanted the book stopped and they wanted their sand returned.

The heirs lost their case. The judge ruled that it was nowhere forbidden to Jae to return from the beach with a few grains of sand in her shoes. The heirs had argued that if everyone carted off their sand, all the sand could disappear and the beach would no longer be beautiful or have any value. The judge may have rolled her eyes, but she ruled that no more than twenty grains of sand per person per visit to the beach could be removed.

The heirs prevailed, to some extent, in the matter of credits: whoever took away any sand would have to credit the heirs in all future uses of the material, including facsimiles and reproductions of same.

Jae's publisher modified the book to include the required credit for the sand in the painting. A copy of the revised book was sent to the heirs. It was returned with the following notations: the painting needed to be altered; the credit needed to be worded in a different way.

The publisher was exasperated. She dictated a curt letter to the heirs, informing them that the book was going forth as it stood. On receiving the letter, the heirs were incensed. They decided to take the matter back to court.

Meanwhile, the government determined that the beach was vital for classified purposes, and revoked the heir's ownership.

This, too, the heirs are disputing. Both cases are pending in the courts and the book is on hold.

Object of Desire

I CONSIDER A LIE TO BE A METAPHOR for the truth. An offering to others for their use according to their need. Yet I am a woman who is often misunderstood, treated like some sort of criminal. This cannot be true: if my actions were crimes, surely more of them would succeed. I persevere in the face of great hardship, for it is the only thing I know how to do.

I find myself to have promised something to someone. She is decent, reasonably satisfied with what she believes me to be. The Beautician works in a shop; sells cosmetics, soaps. Her hues and scents, all strong, change daily. I had wandered into the shop without purpose. We talked at length, that is, I talked, she listened. From the start she called me Honey. The word found a place of loneliness in me like a heat-seeking missile.

She is good to me. She cooks, which is probably why I made the promise. It seemed to be the next thing to do. She has an apartment in town. Inside lurks dark furniture and the troubled eye of her television. She does not approve of my cabin in the woods and hints that I should move in with her. I am considering it. I had despaired and wished for someone constant, someone undemanding.

Her mother became ill; the Beautician left to take care of her. We telephone and write letters. I'm not sure when she will return.

I was introduced to a woman at a concert in town. After the concert I saw her across the room, laughing and gesturing with her hands. The curve of her arms overwhelmed me. Something visited me, surprisingly strong. I sauntered over, began my campaign. I pursued and pursued and now we are lovers.

I call her the Social Worker. She has an earnest look, wears no adornments. I feel strong passion for her. She has begun to complain about the promise, wants me to rescind it. I try to explain that I have given my word, that things must take their course.

The Social Worker, in her resourceful way, decided that we should go to therapy together. I felt horror at the idea but it was easier to go along than to refuse. We went to a psychiatrist in an expensive office. The psychiatrist seemed very sure of herself, talked a lot. I looked at the bland watercolors on her wall. By concentrating very hard on the paintings, I managed not to hear what she was saying. The Social

Worker was weeping from time to time, as she does. The psychiatrist seemed unmoved by her tears; she struck me as callous. I considered getting angry at her but thought better of it. She asked us to come back. Neither of us wanted to. The Social Worker dropped me off at my cabin, gunned her engine, and drove away in frustration. I felt a pang of guilt. I noticed that I needed groceries and drove to town.

I was standing in line at the grocery store, reading the tabloid headlines. One about the world's largest woman caught my eye: "Sixteen Hundred Pounds, a Complete Recluse." Within was a photograph. The picture was blurred, dim. Next to it was a photo of a house, an arrow showing the window through which the other picture had been taken. My heart began to pound. Impossible, but still, I could swear I recognized the house! There was no mention of where it was. I bought the paper and went home.

Up the dirt road past my cabin, winding through the shadowy canyon, I came to a house, compared it with the photo. The same! Same trees, same bushes, same window! The curtain was drawn. I circled the house, listening. Silence. Could it be that within was the world's biggest woman?

Obsession. Of course that it what it is. I walk up

the road to her house. Check every window. I have become familiar with the sound of the creek—the same creek that runs by my cabin—the sighing wind, the scraping branches.

I heard something. Footsteps. I was tremendously excited. A creaking of floorboards, a slowness, like a weight carefully lowered and lifted. Where was she going? I waited a long time. Nothing more.

I have looked at her picture a thousand times. Frankly, it is a terrible photograph. There appears to be some shape, some outline of something. Light against dark, faintly. Perhaps a shoulder dimming into grayness. I went to the library for information. Other famous large women were mentioned, none in my town.

So there she is, the world's heaviest woman, just up the road from me. I visit her house every day in secret. I dream of her. Dream of her body. Dream of her slow careful steps. Dream of her mind.

I long to meet her. I want to capture her interest. What could possibly draw her to me?

It is so simple to imagine, so heroic in its ambition and demands: I will become her equal. I shall weigh in the hundreds of pounds, wearing my garment of flesh proudly. She shall see me well-lit, my form defined. Then she shall come to me, just down the road, where I await her in nuptial white. For I am already in love with her. She consumes my days.

I have taken to eating the richest food I can bear, devising recipes: baguettes dripping with olive oil, sprinkled with parmesan and herbs; a fudge made with butter, chocolate, and nuts; barbecued meats, ribs laden with fat. It is not my nature to eat this way. My tastes are simple, even austere. For my love I seek out fats and oils and stuff myself as much as I can. Already I have gained twenty pounds. My clothes are tight. I welcome them, mortifications of the body, reminding me of my devotions.

The Social Worker has already noticed the change. I stay away from her as much as possible but she plies me with goodwill and aid that cannot always be avoided.

When I go into town I observe the larger people, my rivals: some with swaying gaits, others with light, graceful steps; some hiding under flapping garments, others seemingly oblivious of flesh pushing between buttons, straining seams, bursting them; a few proud ones in beautiful dresses. I disdain the essentially thin with a round paunch in front. I admire those with wide hips, thick necks, the achievement of overall proportion.

I despair. My scales have been holding at two hundred pounds. Still, the weight has gone on nicely. I am surrounded by an even layer of fat. Since I am growing like a child, I am buying clothes secondhand to save money. But I have already found a seamstress who specializes in giants in height and weight. There will I go when the time is right. There will I go for my wooing suit.

I almost had to laugh today when the Social Worker was ministering to me. She assumes that my increase in size emanates from despair. She wants to hurl herself into the fray. Help me to diet, exercise, get to the bottom of what is troubling me. The greater her concern, the more I know I am succeeding. To please her, I pretend to be grateful, nod agreement with her regimens. Yet I see no diminution in her zeal at lovemaking; if anything, she seems more ardent than before. As, I confess, am I, when my large body presses against her thin one. In those moments I forget the Beloved and half-consider the Social Worker's plans for me, imagining what it would be like to be rehabilitated. It is pleasurable, like being a child in the care of a strong, well-intentioned mother. Once she leaves I am master of my fate again, back to my visits, my recipes, my dreams.

The scales registered an increase of seven pounds! The end of my plateau and the greatest advance of any twenty-four hour period. My body, seemingly intransigent and against me, was, in fact, preparing for this leap.

Walking has become more difficult. I find myself panting as I move up the road. Every warrior suffers wounds; I shall bear mine proudly.

I thought further about the matter of stamina. If I am to succeed, endurance will be necessary. I have started an exercise program. Already I feel more powerful, more statuesque.

Three hundred pounds. Now I cut quite a figure. Ah, Beloved, are you peering out at me from behind your curtain? Do you see my progress, do you understand what I am doing for love of you?

The thought that she might be watching both thrills and worries me. It would be wonderful if sympathy were already developing in her heart, if she sees and approves of my design. But if she knows of me, what does she think of this devotee who walks the perimeter of her house every day, who stands next to windows and doors, listening. I shall embark on a new plan: I must, at all times, stand more proudly, must move with more grace and confidence. I must begin wearing attractive clothes despite the expense. On the other hand, if she does not know of my presence, I shall still be stealthy. For I am not yet worthy of her. I have pounds and pounds to go before I can kiss the hem of her garment. The Beloved keeps me humble. In town only one other surpasses me. But we are fledglings compared to the great woman.

I am beginning to have rolls of flesh on my abdomen, two of them. I have smooth pale skin. The rolls remind me of something at dim sum, beautifully rounded like pork buns. Through long practice I have become able to consume a drink I call hot rummed butter: a few drops of dark rum added to a cup of melted butter, a dash of brown sugar. This has accelerated my progress. Also, it mellows me. In the evening before bed, I drink one or two. Then I fall into sound, soft sleep.

A letter today from the Beautician. She writes that she misses me, will try to come out soon for a visit. I begin to think everything will work out. Her orientation to beauty is of a particular type. She will probably break the promise when she sees me. I must remember not to wear my new white dress or navy suit when she arrives. In them I am altogether too dazzling.

The Social Worker is getting worked up about the

impending visit. She wants me to call off the promise. I keep reassuring her that there is nothing to worry about. Since the Social Worker wants to believe it, she does. Also, I am quite convincing when I say this woman poses no threat. As for the Beloved, she is a force of nature. Some things carry earth and all our feeble structures along in their power. One cannot be held responsible for what comes to pass in their wake.

The Beautician's mother took a turn for the worse; the visit was cancelled with regret and apologies. I was gracefully consoling.

The Social Worker calmed down. She looked quite victorious when she heard the news.

We celebrated. She seems to be abandoning her weight loss mission for me. I think she assumes my size will discourage any rivals. I don't have the heart to tell her my secret. Perhaps she has guessed and is keeping silent for her own reasons. In which case it would be cruel to force her to discuss what she has chosen to avoid.

Four hundred pounds. How wide my neck has become, my face is huge. Has anyone made the connection between my transformation and the woman up the road? Apparently not. All over town I ask whether there are other large women nearby. A few are mentioned, never the Beloved. Her obscurity increases our bond.

The path of the pilgrim is relentless in its demand for faith and works. I faltered, contacted the person who did the story for the tabloid, a young reporter in the city. She was willing to meet at her favorite bar if I would buy the drinks.

The Reporter began to relax after a few shots of expensive scotch. I, too, cushioned myself with liquor, then asked about the Beloved. I had not realized how much strain I was under, keeping my secret, creating a chasm between me and all of humanity.

The Reporter drank until she could receive my confession with sympathy. Then she told me one of her best sources had given her the tip.

She drove to the Beloved's house, went up to the front door, knocked. No answer. Knocked again. No answer. Pounded on the door and asked loudly if anyone were home. She thought she heard a creak, then a faint voice asking, "Who is it?" She explained her purpose. The voice said, "Go away." She scouted around outside the house, saw the open window, dashed up, snapped the photographs, and left.

The photos! My hands trembled as I took them from her. Views of the house and the shots through the window. The form I knew so well. Yet clearer! Even in the dimness of the bar I could see the Beloved's shoulder; above it, probably draping hair; below, probably torso. The face was in shadow, or perhaps it was the back of her head. Above the figure was a wall with a framed picture of a landscape, very faint.

Was there anything else? What about the source? No, that was confidential. I begged, offered a lot of money. Finally the Reporter said she would try to arrange a meeting between the source and me, but it was unlikely. She sold me the photos for a few hundred dollars. We drank some coffee.

I arrived at my cabin as the sun rose—a moment of grace in my exhausting quest.

The Social Worker had left several messages, sounding more worried each time, begging me to call her as soon as I came home. I did, even invited her over. We spent the morning making love, the afternoon sleeping in each other's arms. I felt close to her. Talking to the Reporter, possessing the photographs, had helped to ease a sorrow. The Social Worker lay curled against me like a baby. I watched her tenderly. I felt worthy of being loved, not something I try to think about too often.

Six hundred pounds. I have triumphed over everyone in town. Only my hidden love surpasses me. I am confident now. I have found a way to reliably gain at least a pound a day. At this rate, I shall be ready in less than three years. I have yet another navy blue suit, a dress like a ship's new sail. Rolls of fat hide my neck; plump flesh hangs from my arms, piles on the backs of my wrists, the tops of my feet. My abdomen is immense—proud and wide and rolled. My hair shines, my nails grow quickly, my eyes are clear.

In town, people stand aside to let me pass. They see my imposing bearing, my stateliness, my level gaze. They are confounded in the presence of such mystery. I am treated with great care, seen as something almost more than human, almost to be worshipped. Still, I am burdened by my solitude. Knights of old grew lonely in the forest.

The Reporter called. The source was nearby and wanted to stop in. She was willing to answer a few questions in return for an interview. I hurriedly cleaned my cabin, showered, put on my white dress. My guests arrived.

The Source was thin as a mantis. Her dark eyes penetrated me. I served food and whiskey, drank quickly in order to calm myself before those eyes.

She asked many questions. At first I didn't want to talk about the Beloved at all. I felt embarrassed. But it seemed my only hope for some sort of exchange. The Source did not blink as she listened to my story. She was my inquisitor, laying bare my desire in her cold gaze. When all my secrets were revealed, the Reporter reminded her that I had agreed to the meeting in order to gain information for myself.

The Source nodded and began. She had her own source. I interrupted to ask about it. She gave a twitch of irritation and continued. The Beloved is believed to be the world's largest woman but she is a complete recluse. Thus, she is not mentioned in books of world records or medical articles. The Source noted that many of the world's greatest achievers are in seclusion and virtually unknown. The Reporter's photographs are the only ones known to exist.

She started to tell me some details of the Beloved's life. Suddenly overcome with doubt and fear, I cried out that I had heard enough. I begged them to leave. Then, exhausted from whiskey and my ordeal, I lay down and fell asleep.

I was awakened by sights and sounds in the darkness—sirens and flashing lights. Instantly I was alert, terrified. The Beloved!

I struggled to rise, stepped into slippers, and went outside. Flashlights bobbed in the road.

"See that?"

"What?"

"Some lady fell back there. Think she may of gotten trampled, haw haw."

I recognized the voices of my neighbors. We hurried along behind the roaring machines. All up the road the crowd increased. People in bathrobes. People carrying beer bottles. Beside me was a teenage girl on crutches.

"Hey, Gigantica Hugica." The teenager attempted to make conversation.

I grunted, too preoccupied for speech.

"Lend you a crutch if you need it."

I shook my head.

Closer to the Beloved's house we came. I was almost swooning with exertion and dread. What's this? Fire engine not there? Gone further ahead, not her house at all!

I staggered and sank down onto the road, could not stop the tears that fell with relief. The others turned to me in concern.

"Need a hand?" asked the teenager.

"Big gal must of tripped on something. Call the

fire department, haw haw," joked someone behind me.

I gasped for them to go on, I would be alright. The group continued up the road.

I arose, drew nearer to the Beloved's house. Its very walls reassured me, solid in the night's gloom.

Then, miracle of miracles. A light went on. I heard the sound of creaking, creaking. Coming closer until, yes, the front door slowly opened. I had no flashlight, could not be seen in the darkness.

There she was in all her magnificence, silhouetted behind the doorframe. I could see how softly rippled was her flowing hair, with what quiet grace she stood and peered out. Her body filled the doorway and disappeared on either side. I saw in reality the worshipped curve of shoulder.

I could not help myself. "Beloved," I whispered, my deepest passion compressed into that single word. I saw her head turn, majestically, toward my voice.

A second time the word came forth, unbidden: "Beloved." I took a step toward her.

And this—this was my triumph. For though she said nothing, though the door began to close, it was slowly, slowly, thoughtfully.

I am fortified. I shall complete my holy preparation. I shall win her.

Philosophie, Thinly Clothed

PHILOSOPHIE LIVED IN A QUARTZ-LINED cave, high on the side of a mountain. Her life was one of solitude and contentment.

A time came, however, when some determined citizens climbed up the mountainside to see her. They begged her to come down into their city so that the populace might learn from her. At length she agreed.

She was welcomed with enthusiasm wherever she went: the market, the amphitheater, or simply lounging with young women on the wide steps of the city's most beautiful building. Questions were asked, answers given, more questions asked.

Philosophie was a pleasure to look upon, tall and muscular. Sculptors begged her to pose for them. She discovered that she enjoyed having her body gazed upon, even scrutinized. Several magnificent statues were carved.

Everyone was pleased with her visit. With a feeling of satisfaction she returned to her mountain home.

Many years later a group of petitioners from a different city arrived at her cave, saying there was strife among the people. Her assistance was desperately needed to help bring about order and tranquility.

Philosophie was striding down a wide boulevard but no one smiled or stopped her to engage in conversation. In fact, the glances directed her way were quizzical or frankly disapproving. She heard a piercing, high-pitched sound.

"Halt! You're under arrest!" shouted a uniformed woman.

"Why?" asked Philosophie.

"You must know you can't go around naked. It's against the law."

Did I mention that Philosophie had never worn clothes? Neither in her cave nor in the other city, where her body had been regarded as a pleasure, even an inspiration, to look upon.

She saw a clothing shop across the street and promised to get something to wear. She emerged from the store fully dressed, not feeling like herself at all.

Continuing her walk, she noticed a statue in front of a large building. It was a copy of one for which she had posed during her visit to the other city. Now here she was, grand and naked. The people walking past seemed not to mind, a few even glanced up in admiration.

Later, talking with some artists and professors at a

café, she could scarcely believe what they were saying—they were complimenting her on her clothes! She tried to steer the conversation to more important matters but her efforts were in vain.

On the boulevard a few days later, she noticed a shop where fabric was sold. Inside she discovered a bolt of diaphanous cloth. She bought a length and took it to a seamstress.

She put on her beautiful new dress. It draped closely over her body. Furthermore, while from certain angles one could not see through the material, from other angles one could. It was not as comfortable as nudity, but it was an improvement over her other clothes.

Leaving the seamstress, she stepped out onto the boulevard. Several university students were approaching. On seeing Philosophie they frowned and started to mutter about the disgraceful transparent dress.

Philosophie turned slightly and the dress became opaque.

"What just happened?" murmured the students.

Philosophie seized on their confusion to press the purpose of her visit: questions were asked, answers given, more questions asked. But after a few minutes, the students' minds began to wander.

So Philosophie turned and again the students could

see through the dress. "What's going on? We don't understand," complained the students. There was another moment of bewilderment, another opportunity for Philosophie to pursue her aim.

And when that began to flag, she turned again.

Person by person and group by group, she continued her encounters throughout the city. She used the dress—transparent and opaque, opaque and transparent—each time.

Progress was slow. She had to stay on and on. In fact, she is there to this day, still trying to finish her task.

Acknowledgments

I will always be grateful to Julius Young, who dissuaded me from my goal of posthumous publication. My heartfelt thanks to Jeffrey Miller, inimitable editor and publisher. My deep appreciation to Bruce Washbish and Colleen Dwire of the Anchor & Acorn Press, S. N. Walker of Walker Studio, and everyone who has helped to bring this book forth. I hope you know who you are.

This
first edition
of *Philosophie
Thinly Clothed* has been
printed and bound by McNaughton
& Gunn. Text composed and
set in Baskerville. Design
by Jeffrey Miller